HEXED

Jeni Burns

Hexed

Twisted Fate Novella #4

Copyright © 2015

Jeni Burns

c/o Media Jam

15105-D John J. Delaney Drive; #317

Charlotte, NC 28277

Cover Design By: Indira Jainanan

http://www.indirajartwork.com/

Print ISBNs
ISBN: 1-942964-09-9
ISBN-13: 978-1-942964-09-4

Acknowledgements:

Every new book brings more people to thank to the table. So, in order to save time:

Thank you to all my writer friends who constantly offer their experience, knowledge, and inspiration. Love you guys.

Thank you to my friends and family—the list being longer than my body. You all know who you are and how much I love you.

Thanks to the amazing folks at my favorite coffee shop, Rush Espresso in Charlotte, NC. You all keep me working.

Thanks to Lara Stokes, Reagan Phillips, Kim Ford, Denise Leton, Natalie Ratcliffe, Sophia Henry, Lauriel Faltin, Shaila Patel, and Josh Strecker for beta reading, critiquing, and believing in me. You guys rock.

Thanks to Darynda Jones for reminding me to kick it up a notch and telling me I started in the wrong place. The book is better because of you.

Thanks to Melissa Shank for taking the time to not only read, comment, and make suggestions that made this a better book, but also for being a good friend when I really needed one. I'm eternally grateful.

Thanks to Indira Jainanan for taking my few lines of description and turning it into a fabulous cover. Your talent amazes me.

Thanks to everyone who helped edit including, Jan Carol, Help Me Edit Editing Services, and Joshua Strecker.
Without them, this book would be a punctuation and continuity nightmare.

Thank you to all my friends and family who have stood behind me and cheered me along this journey. To Sophia Henry who sits beside me working so hard that I have no choice but to work at least half as hard as she does. To Lara Stokes for early morning breakfast chats and late night walk and talks. To Taz Shahpurwala who will answer my texts at midnight to reassure me this next book won't suck. To Dee Lorenzo for suggesting a night in with girl talk and wine so I can escape from the characters in my head. To George Lauer for always having the right tools to fix my plot holes from 600 miles away and who will invite me to crash family functions when I'm away from home so I never feel alone. My love for every one of you runs deep.

And last, but surely not least, thank you to my readers. Without you, my job would be meaningless.

With all my thanks,
~ j

To Denise Leton.

For everything you do (and I mean everything).

This journey is worth taking with you beside me.

ONE

SHADOWS SURROUNDED DRAMMELECH like a cloak outside the Daily Dews coffee shop and bookstore. The turmoil within its walls sent a perverse sense of joy streaming through his body. A smile split his lips despite not being in his nature. Taking possession of the witch with his sister's name proved a worthwhile juncture, even if only for the entertainment value she brought him. Why those grown men fawned and fought over Calliope Dewsberry boggled his mind, but anytime men were pitted against one another until the strongest prevailed, he found satisfaction.

Had he been human, those notions would make him a monster among men, but him? Human? *No.* He was the being of nightmares. The spawn of true evil. A devil. No. *The devil.* The moniker 'Jersey Devil' became his centuries ago and he wore it with pride, hoping to earn his father's respect.

His smile widened. *Dear old dad;* a devil of the highest order. One who gave him more than life. He'd provided him with purpose. A calling. As the kids these days said, *goals.*

Drammelech turned his attention back to the large bay window of the store and rubbed his hands together, the itch to intervene growing with every second. His mission bordered on completion. The witch swore to serve him if he promised to spare the two men she cared for, thus ensuring the key to the Overworld would be his. He cocked his head and stared at the *humans*, the word acid on his tongue.

What was she waiting for? The orders had been clear. Go inside and convince Daphne Barren to willingly join them. If she did, Calliope wouldn't spell the men into fighting—to the death, he allowed the witch to wrongly assume. Death would be too simple. Uncomplicated. Clean. No. Drammelech relished the knowledge the fight would be over her. Maybe to the death for fun. *His* fun.

Laughter tickled his trachea. The third man inside sweetened the deal. He agreed the Barren boys would go unharmed as long as Calliope did as commanded, but this other man created a loophole he didn't see coming. An advantage he'd keep in his back pocket for the exact right moment. These little twists were what he lived for. Based on the glances shooting between Calliope and the man, they were in love. And not the love she had for the twins either. *Real* love. The kind that, when gone, ripped out hearts and fed them to demons. Demons like him—and he was starving.

Now he possessed something even more valuable: leverage.

Tired of waiting, he sent a mental push to Calliope, forcing her hand. Without such pressure, she aimed for a solution to save her precious friends. Which made the scene unfolding inside even more enticing for him to behold. Compulsion at its finest.

Amused, he stared, as the unknown male pummeled Dax Barren, the triplet who hand delivered a quartz amulet to him on the promise he would allow him to see his mother. His mother's body laid in a medical facility hooked up to machines because she had offered him, the Jersey Devil, her pure soul in exchange for postponing her daughter's servitude. A postponement which neared its end. In fact, if memory served, she and her brothers would be turning twenty-six soon. Most young people were prone to parties and celebrations for such milestones, but these youngsters would mourn the loss of their sister. *Daphne*. The key to everything.

A true smile danced across his face. It wouldn't be much longer, and everything he needed to cement his rightful place as the ruler of these people would be his. If the words of his father from his youth were to be believed, he would stand to rule the Overworld, bending all beings to his will, until they all bowed before him and did his bidding. Bored with the standoff between the three men vying for the female witch's affections, he allowed himself the respite of dreams. Dreams of a world where humans worshiped at his altar and did as he commanded. Free will would be a memory from the past and he would enjoy his reign of power.

But what he most enjoyed imagining was his father. The man who brought him into existence and raised him in his image. Who suffered for hundreds of years in the Underworld where another bitch of a witch banished him. The time since he'd last had the luxury of even a conversation with the man was so long ago, it was all but removed from his mind. Except for the sentiment, "witches can't be trusted." Moreover, they deserved to be exterminated. They didn't merit a place in the Overworld. Their souls belonged firmly ensconced in the fiery pits of hell, where their magic could hurt no one. Only then would he and his father walk together in glory.

Proud.

Strong.

Unbeatable.

Emotion swelled in his gut and threatened to wind its way into his heart, where he refused to allow it entry. Cheap human emotion didn't belong in his world. All it would do is deter him from achieving the greatness he knew awaited him.

A crash inside the bookstore pulled Drammelech back into the present, his dreams and ambitions solidly settled into the center of his being. The male grabbed the middle brother in a headlock and the older one captured Drammelech's witch in a passionate embrace she fought with all her energy. This would be a night Calliope would regret for the rest of her days. Drammelech smiled. The compulsion bestowed on her was as effective as he'd imagined it would be. A guilt-free craving tended to bring out the worst in humans.

With strength he never imagined she possessed, she wriggled free from Nic Barren, kneed him in the groin, and turned fiery eyes on the other two struggling males. Drammelech observed, unable to turn away from the train wreck in progress, as Calliope spelled both Dax and the man who he believed to be her current flame before turning her intentions on Nic, who writhed on the ground. A smile tugged again at his lips as he offered the witch a mental push full of his intention.

Both men dropped like stones in water, sank to the floor motionless and wide-eyed while Nic stilled. Pride surged through Drammelech with the ferocity of a freight train headed downhill without brakes. Who would've guessed one of his mother's descendants would be able, no, *willing*, to dip into their dark magic resources all on their own. It hadn't been in his mental suggestion, but he approved her choice. He withdrew his power and waited. She whirled toward something invisible to him, but the panic in her eyes betrayed her.

Ah, the reason for his assault finally showed herself. Made herself vulnerable. Weak. *Human.*

"Come on. This is what you're here for," he

cooed aloud to himself as he waited for what the witch would do next. The scene played in front of him like a telenovela with the sound turned all the way down. Calliope gestured wildly. Stomped her foot. Bit her lip. Shook her head, slow, as if resignation sank in.

Excitement bubbled inside as Drammelech rubbed his hands together. *This was it.* He'd take possession of Daphne and keep her until her birthday rolled around. On that day, and not a day sooner, he would release her mother's soul back into her decaying body. Whoever remained of her family would be too engrossed in the apparent miracle to stop him. The key to the Overworld would be his, and the woman they cried over would be theirs—well, as much as they could enjoy a walking corpse. Laughter spilled out of him, unbidden and harsh. The taste of his victory erupted on his dual-tipped tongue.

What was taking Calliope so long? The seconds ticking by annoyed him. Daphne should be ready to leave either on her own or under a compulsion by now. He moved closer to the glass windowpane and peered inside. He scanned for Daphne but found her nowhere. What was going on? The shop didn't offer many hiding places.

He leaned in closer. Frustration and anger warred for dominance within him. Neither got to take command. The pane of glass beneath his fingertips and face exploded into thousands of tiny razor sharp shards aimed for his tender skin. With a shriek, he fell to the sidewalk, covered his face, and hissed in pain. He slunk into the darkness to lick his wounds but didn't go far, because he knew they weren't done yet.

This was it.

The last straw.

The final nail in the coffin.

The Barrens were as good as dead.

TWO

"I'D HATE TO be on your bad side," Jason Clarks whispered as the devil's shrill shrieks split the night.

"Hush," Callie reprimanded. "He's not gone yet. Play dead or something."

"Playing dead is my middle name," he quipped in a low tone. The magical compulsion Callie sent their way earlier still made Jason shiver with need. Without a doubt, the intention behind the spell focused on desire. Why, he couldn't be sure, but it seemed the devil planned to cause as much trouble as possible in every aspect of her life.

Her strength grew with every spell and soon combating what she so flawlessly tossed his way with or without Drammelech's assistance would be impossible. And yet, here he laid, on the cold, hard floor of her family shop, wanting nothing more than to grab her in his arms and make good on the promise he made. The promise to keep safe the only thing the devil wanted.

He shook the thought from his mind. Daphne was tucked away upstairs in Callie's apartment with be-spelled charms keeping guard. So long as no one meaning her harm attempted to enter the building, everything would be fine.

"I think he's gone."

"We really got him good." He rose to his feet and rubbed the sore spot on the back of his head. "Although I wasn't expecting Nic to hit me." He shot a pointed look at the man laying on the floor at Callie's feet. He swung his eyes back toward Dax. The man sat on his knees and rubbed his chin. The satisfaction of landing a punch on the man's smug face radiated through him. Tough guy? What tough guy?

"I'm sure Elech will make me pay for our stunt," Callie mused aloud as she moved toward Jason. "I shouldn't be here. I should've found a way to resist. To fight him. To protect all of you."

Disappointment clung to her words and ripped a chasm inside him. "Tell him I conjured the window to break." He reached for her. "Don't you dare let him hurt you for this. It was my idea." Honeysuckle and brimstone toyed with his senses as he wrapped her in the security of his embrace. He'd spent sixty-nine years imprisoned in stained glass at the hands of his last witchy woman and yet her powers didn't compare to the magical current he sensed in Callie. Much like his own lineage, hers must be tied to an impressive ancestor. Not many of the craft could withstand the devil's compulsion long enough to allow for a counterattack, minor as it was.

"He was there when you broke out of your window," she chided. "Do you really think he's dumb enough to believe I didn't have a hand in this, after witnessing what happened there?"

The way her head tilted to the side and her shoulders fell, made him want to steal her away, run as far from here and the Barren triplets as possible. To protect her from the blasted devil. A woman like her deserved normalcy, and he wanted to be the man to give it to her. The remnants of her compulsion still tugged at him. But he didn't dare credit her spell when his hand wound deep into her hair and his lips kissed her senseless. Every passing second was all him. All male. All wanting. And if it was all wrong, he could die, happy, never being right again.

She tasted of peaches and sunlight as his tongue slipped past the seam of her lips. The press of her body against his, a haven in the chaos of the day's events, he longed to escape into for the rest of forever. But the sound of a throat clearing stopped him short.

"Screw this. I'm getting out of here. When you decide to finally pick a man who's capable of loving you the way you deserve, call me."

Jason pulled away from Callie as Nic stomped out of the store area, his devil-do-his-worst attitude firmly intact. He almost felt bad for the guy. Not only had Nic woken up in the back of his own car at the Dews and found his brother and some guy fighting over the woman he's probably loved from afar his entire life, but the swift kick to the groin delivered by said woman… He shook his head. There was no getting around the fact he'd never give up on Callie, not even for Nic and his puppy dog crush. Not while he still had the ability to draw breath into his lungs.

Jason froze. If the devil was ready for round two, he was screwed. A quick assessment did little to calm his double baked nerves. Callie appeared ready to come unglued, Dax appeared on the verge of slitting someone's throat—maybe even his own—and upstairs behind a damn wind chime, sat the object of the devil's desire. *Shit.*

"What the hell happened?" Dax stood and turned his glare on him.

"Dax, I'm so sorry." Callie hiccuped.

"Sorry for what, Opie? I did this to you. I got you into this and I'll get you out of it." He scratched at his unruly hair, a haunted look on his face. "Maybe a good night's sleep will help? A fresh start." He moved closer to Callie. Reached for her.

Dax's use of his childhood nickname for Callie irritated Jason to no end. "As long as you understand you aren't sleeping here," he challenged, insinuating himself between the two.

Dax shot him with a glare. "Whatever you say, buddy."

Jason clenched his hands into fists at his sides,

ready to hit Dax again. If it took the smugness off his face, it'd be worth it. He cracked his neck and rose to the balls of his feet.

"Guys, don't argue. I can't stay here either. If I do, it makes all of you vulnerable to Elech."

Jason sighed as Callie hugged her arms around herself, the truth of her words chilling. She turned to him, eyes full of regret and longing.

"You promised you'd protect Daphne. Me being here will only make it complicated. I can't be sure Elech won't control me and compel me to do something I won't be able to resist." She reached a hand to Jason's cheek.

"Calliope Jane." Her name was a hymn on his lips. "I doubt there is much the devil could make you do. You were able to convince him Daphne was in here." As the other woman's name left his lips, a sinking feeling settled deep in the pit of his stomach. "You aren't here for Daphne, are you?" He stepped back, the absence of her caress stood in stark contrast to the clang of warning bells ringing in his head. The woman he knew and cared for, regardless of how recent their connection, wouldn't do something as devious as make him trust her only to stab him in the back. *Would she?*

Jason studied Callie's face, and the nagging in the back of his mind tugged again. Something was off. He scrubbed a hand across his chin and contemplated how to proceed.

"Maybe Daphne is tired of running," Callie hedged. "Maybe she wants to come out and talk to me about all this. Elech has been a monster in many ways. I'm not defending him, but so far, he's treated me okay. Not like he did to Hope all those years ago. And honestly, Hope was the one who made the deal with him. She *willingly* gave up her soul. We need to keep it all in perspective. Right?"

Words stuck in Jason's throat as every warning signal in his body flashed bright and bold.

Dax argued, "My mother gave her soul for Daphne's freedom. She wanted her to live a normal life."

He stepped closer to Callie and Jason's sense of better judgment went into overdrive.

This wasn't right. Minutes ago, the honor of biggest threat in the building belonged to Dax, but there was no mistaking the subtle shift. Dax was the last one Jason expected to argue with Callie. "Callie, I think maybe you're right. It's time for you to go," he suggested, standing his ground, solid and stoic. When she didn't move toward the door, he began the silent work of conjuring salt from the break room. The grains crept across the floor like white ants and settled around him in a thin circle.

"Dax, I don't think Callie is feeling herself," he warned. "Maybe you should come over here and join me."

Dax turned his stormy blue eyes on Jason and narrowed them. "Opie and I have a long history. The kind you can't jump into in a matter of hours."

His open hatred slashed Jason.

"I'm not arguing with you. I just think you might want to reconsider." Jason raised his brow and cocked his head, hoping that Dax would read more into the words he was saying, but the man was either completely clueless or downright ignorant. The only good thing about the interlude was it had captured Callie's attention, and she hadn't seen the salt circle. If Jason couldn't get Dax into the damn circle on his own, then there wasn't anything more he could do.

His fingers twitched by his side. He needed a spell to defend against whatever Callie would send his way. A witch of her caliber would try something. That he didn't doubt. What spell, he didn't know. His instincts might be rusty, but he trusted them on this. Almost as much as he trusted them when they screamed she was the woman for him. Even if right now she was about to do something he wasn't going to like.

Something bad.

There wasn't a warning before it came. The spell seeped into existence without a shift in the air around them. There was no time for either man to move out of her line of fire. Fire being the word of the moment since it was the only way to describe how it felt when her spell beat against the protective barrier. Heated flames of desire. Hot and heavy, demanding things of him he'd typically give without hesitation. But there was nothing good coming out of the heated desire spell she wove. Not for him. Not for Dax. And definitely not for her, since he was immune in his shelter.

Callie's mouth flew open and a string of curses left her lips in the most unladylike way imaginable. Dax stared at her, confusion etched on his face.

Why wasn't the spell sending him on his hands and knees to do her bidding? A passion spell of this caliber should have a man so infatuated with her crawling across the floor ready to do whatever she commanded. Dax kicked the toe of his boot into the floorboards and slid the personal telephone people these days carried from his pocket. He shot Callie an odd look and pressed buttons on the hand-held device before moving it to his ear.

"Maureen? Yeah, it's me. Can you come to the Dews? I need to see you."

Callie's bottom lip dropped even wider, and the curses stopped mid-stream. "You piece of shit." She whirled on Jason and gave him a dark stare as if weighing the words about to leave her lips. "Did you do this? Did you make him call *her*?"

Before he could get another word in edgewise, Nic strode through the doorway separating the store from the break room. "Do you have any leftover Chinese upstairs? All of a sudden I'm craving egg rolls and wonton soup. I *know* you like wonton soup." His fixed stare sent a wash of confusion over Callie's face.

"No, but there might be a menu in the break room," she hedged.

Nic nodded and left with a spring in his step. Jason gave a small, silent shake of his head before raising his shoulders in surrender. "Spells oftentimes have unexpected consequences, darling." He arched a brow and considered whether to probe further into the wounded tone of her accusations.

"I understand you're busy, but I *need* you. *Now*." Dax's words grew louder in the awkward silence surrounding them. "Dammit, Maureen. I don't see what's got you so busy this time of night. Never mind." Dax stabbed at the screen of his phone, dropped it back into his pocket, and turned toward the rear of the building. "Sorry, Opie. I've gotta run. Something to take care of. See you later?" The quick dismissal and clipped phrases sent a spread of redness up Callie's face until they landed with a full flush in her cheeks and the bridge of her nose.

When Dax cleared the curtain between the store and the break room, Callie turned to Jason, hatred hot in her haunted eyes.

"I'm not sure what you did, you bastard, but I'll make you pay for it." Her eyes glowered in the fluorescent lighting.

"Pay for what? Making the man you beat off you earlier *not* want you? Let's be honest, Callie, he wasn't the one you wanted groveling at your feet, was he? And you're only upset because we both didn't fall victim to your damn passion spell." He cut his eyes at the woman, trying to ignore how her blond curls surrounded her face like a halo. She wasn't innocent. Nor was she sweet. Not if the outrage coming off her in violent waves could be trusted.

"Dax has wanted me forever. He should be dragging Daphne out of her hiding spot by now." Petulant wasn't Callie's color. In fact, it was the first time he'd say she was anything other than beautiful.

"Maybe he's loved you forever," Jason agreed, careful to stay within the delicate salt stream surrounding him on the floor, "but you cast a passion spell, darling. And passion and love don't always go hand in hand," he reasoned. "Sounds to me like good 'ol Dax found someone more suited to him in the bedroom." The barb landed as aimed, and Callie's face crumbled.

"He used me," she whispered.

"As I see it, that knife cuts both ways." As her intentions became clearer, he watched the forgotten charmed chimes wiggle to life, the remnants of his earlier spell sparked. "I think it's time for you to leave, Callie," he suggested.

"I can't leave. Not without Daphne. I don't want to make him mad." Tears bristled in her eyes, threatening to spill.

"Love, there isn't anything I'd like to do more than to take you away from that monster, but if you recall, I made you a promise, and I intend to keep it."

The push of his wards began in earnest now, pulling her like a magnet toward the door. She gave him one last glance, sad and unsure, before she turned her back to him and left.

THREE

ANXIOUS ENERGY ENVELOPED Dax without warning.
Jason sure looked pretty damn smug back there
and it pissed him off. Hell, he'd spent most of his
life fighting with Nic over Opie, and now this guy
wanted a piece of the action? Oh, hell no.

Yet, the ache in his gut wasn't aimed toward
Opie. Instead, it pointed in Maureen's direction
loud and clear even though she was refusing to see
him tonight. *Maybe because you screwed Callie while
you were supposed to be dating her.* The little voice in
the back of his head mocked him.

The need to smash his fist into something
raised its ugly head. Dax tamped it down and tried
to hold onto his cool, at least until he could clear
the building. Before the screen door could bang
behind him, he paced the alleyway behind the
store like a pendulum on a clock. Back and forth.

Back and forth. The hollow thud of his boots on the asphalt reflected the emptiness inside.

There had to be something he could do. This was all his fault. First his mother, then Grams, and now Opie. The only person left was the one standing between him and everyone else being back to normal.

In all of his almost twenty-six years on the planet, he'd heard how special his sister was. *We have to protect Daphne. We can't let the devil get Daphne. Daphne is the only one who can make sure the devil doesn't get control of the world. Daphne, Daphne, Daphne.* His subconscious mimicked a grumpy toddler with a huge me, me, me complex, but Dax didn't care. He was tired of giving a shit about everything and everyone else.

The anger inside boiled over. He needed a release. One that wouldn't come until he'd pummeled the shit out of something and split the skin on his knuckles. The wooden fence separating the small rear parking area from the store next door would have to do.

Like always, his emotions spiraled out of control and he lost count of how many times his fist connected with the damn post. He pounded until a shard of wood pierced his skin, until his tender flesh bled, until the playback reel in his head silenced. If he hand-delivered Daphne to the devil, it could all end.

Sure, Opie might never forgive him, but he'd already proven to her he couldn't be counted on. His dad would never speak to him again, but since he left for college years ago, they barely spoke anyway. As for Nic, well, he'd be pissed. There was no getting around it. But Nic had a level head on his shoulders. So even in his anger, he'd be the most likely to understand his betrayal of their sister.

Dax took a swallow of night air and plucked a wooden shard from the top of his hand. The pain in his hand mingled with the deeper hurt of Daphne's soon-to-be-loss. She didn't deserve whatever Elech had in mind for her. It wasn't like she planned to be the missing puzzle piece of an old prophecy. But she was, and with every refusal against fulfilling it, their combined future became more uncertain. He rolled his shoulders and puffed out his chest. There wasn't anything more to consider. Doing what was right wasn't always easy, but it wasn't any less right when you did it, his conscience chided.

Mind made up, Dax flicked the toothpick-sized shard onto the ground and went through the back door into the private area of the Dews. He needed to talk to his sister. *Now.*

The fluorescent light in the small kitchen-turned-break room cast a harsh light on the linoleum flooring. Daphne sat at the far end of a table, head tucked in the protective cove of her arms, surrounded by none other than Nic and Jason. It struck him as odd that she'd sit there after hiding away earlier. He stepped over the threshold and felt the push of invisible hands, warning him away. A croak escaped his throat when he tried to protest, but nothing more.

"He warned me," Daphne said, raising her head so she could meet his eyes.

Tears streamed down her face and Dax fought to make sense of her words. Try as he might, he couldn't find the ability to speak.

"He said you'd decide to turn me over to the devil." Her eyes burned with the glow of sapphires. "You can't enter, Dax. Not now. Not ever."

Frustration turned to ire. What in the hell was she spouting off about? His sister had lost her mind.

He took a step back and the pressure vanished as did his inability to speak. "What are you talking about?"

"Jason spelled the bells Callie hangs on all the doors. It will keep people with evil intentions out." She rose from her spot at the table and shook away whatever ran through her brain. "He said you'd be the one to sell me out. You'd trade me for her." Her last word was a mere whisper. A breath. A prayer. "You love her, don't you?"

The question struck him as odd, considering Daphne had always pushed him and Callie together, but the answer rose to his lips without needing to contemplate it further. "Yes. I've loved her from the moment I first laid eyes on her," he affirmed, as memories of a snow-blanketed day assaulted him. It hurt to admit how much Opie meant to him—despite the fact another woman waited for him tonight and two men vying for her affections sat before him. "And as much as I love *you*, I can't let her pay a price that only you're capable of paying."

His sister nodded mutely, understanding etched in the fine lines around her mouth. Nic rose to his feet and puffed out his chest, ready for a fight.

"I can't let Opie become what Mom is: a shell of her former self, her soul clamoring to do the bidding of the devil." He thrust out his arms and again met resistance as he breached the threshold of the doorway. "Please, Daphne, let me come in and we can work it out."

"You aren't welcome here. Not anymore."

"Dammit Nic. Of all people, I thought you would understand. Opie didn't ask for this. Yet, she's the one suffering right now."

"And you think our sister should suffer instead?" Nic's question was punctuated with slow, steady footsteps and the distance between them shrank. "Let me get this straight. You already gave Elech what he needed to find Daphne. You stood by while he coerced Callie into a contract. And now you want to turn over our sister because it cleans everything up, nice and neat?" Disgust clung to his every word. "What the fuck is wrong with you?"

Dax refused to stand there and take shit from his brother. He threw himself into the building and waited for the push against him to lessen, but the sensation of walking through hardening cement assaulted him. Every pulse of his nerve endings misfired as he pushed his unresponsive limbs forward.

Jason shot up from the table, eyes wide. "Damn you all!" He grabbed Daphne by the arm and propelled her toward the stairs leading to the apartment. "I need you to hide. Whatever happens, don't you dare come out. Do you understand?"

His sister ducked up the stairs and Jason turned his focus on him. "What do you think you're doing? You won't get past my wards. Hell, even Callie can't get past them now." He tapped the fingers of his right hand against the leg of his slacks as if contemplating something. "If I remove the charm, do you promise not to hurt your sister?"

Dax fought to make his mouth move, his head nod, anything. But everything felt stuck. All he could do was blink, and he doubted it would be enough to convince the witch he'd do anything for a chance to save Opie.

Anything.

*****

Sitting around the break room table with his brother and Jason held little appeal to Dax. Especially when his sister sat tucked away with only a wind chime and a flight of stairs between them.

He didn't stand a chance in Hell at convincing Daphne to come with him unless at least one of the men at the table agreed with him. How hard could it be? They were all reasonable people. Right?

Dax contemplated Jason's spear straight spine

and salty disposition. Well, maybe not all of them were reasonable. Jason's unwelcome presence irked him. The man, an anomaly in his own right as a male witch, didn't belong here. How did getting freed from a curse by Opie make him a player in this game? Did he feel some misplaced sense of obligation to her or something? And why was he so hell-bent on helping Daphne?

The silence in the room hung thick enough to touch. Nic steepled his fingers and dipped his head. *It was now or never.* "Hey, I don't want to start a fight, but we need to discuss how we plan to rescue Opie."

"You were there. You saw what Callie did. I think she's possessed or something." Nic's eyes flashed in all their sapphire glory while the promise of tears sparkled at the corners.

"First thing's first, I need to get some supplies. My magic is rusty. The only way I stand a chance against Callie and Elech are with some potions."

"What kind of potions?"

Dax hated the hint of optimism in Nic's voice.

"I'm not sure. Where's Callie keep her spell book?"

Enough. Dax banged his hands on the table and reopened the cut on his knuckle. "Opie doesn't have a spell book. She isn't a real witch." He refused to get Nic's hopes up because Jason fancied himself powerful. Besides, during all the time he and Opie dated, she never once did a spell, mixed a potion, or so much as picked up a broom. Jason could blame her for what happened in the store before, but he knew the truth. Elech did it. Somehow he must've used her as a conduit or something; it was the only logical explanation.

"I know you believe she isn't a witch, but it isn't true." Jason slid back his chair, rose to his feet, and leaned across the table leaving a few inches between them.

"The day she came to the B & B after you stole her pendant, she was different. Alive for the first time. She could see and hear me. She could see the other ghosts. Hell, she even fought off the devil and saved your sister. Calliope *is* a witch. And a powerful one."

Dax rose to meet him head on, the compulsion to combat, creeping through his cells. He needed this man to stop talking. To go away. To die.

"I refuse to believe Opie's capable of magic." He leaned back and kicked over his chair. "You guys are going to get her killed." Although, if Jason got caught in the mix and went down instead, it wouldn't be the worst thing to happen. One less obstacle between himself and Opie.

Nic sprang to his feet and grabbed at his sleeve. "Dax. Stop and think for a minute. Jason's trying to help. We all want the same thing—Callie back here; safe."

"He's trying to help get her killed, Nic. Why can't you see it?" He slapped his brother's hand away and braced for impact. His brother was nothing if not predictable. By challenging him on Opie, he might as well have declared war. "Opie's off being controlled by the devil and he's here protecting the one person who can end this."

"Daphne's your sister. How can you consider…"

Dax cut Jason off before he could finish. "That's right. She's our sister. And her fate was sealed the moment she was born. She's the answer to some old riddle. The key to the universe. The only thing Elech wants. Why not hand her over and be done with it? She knows what's coming. Why not get it over with? Why not give her best friend a chance to live a happy life?"

"You mean a life with you?"

Nic's question threw him for a loop. "No," he stammered. "Whatever Opie wants. Whatever makes her happy. Whatever is best for her." He couldn't meet his brother's gaze with the lies streaming off his tongue. He'd say what he needed to for Nic's support, but the truth was, happiness only existed with Opie in his life.

Case in point, in the year since they'd split, he'd dated a handful of women and none had cared for him the way she did. Even now, Maureen, the woman who had professed her love to him only a couple of weeks ago, wouldn't answer his calls. She refused to understand when he explained why he never showed up on the night he spent with Opie. The night he realized he'd do anything to get her back. But in the meantime, he needed Maureen's soft reassurances. Not because he was a jerk, but because he was broken. So much so, that no woman would be able to make him whole again. Not without knowing his history. An unbelievable history written long ago by creatures no one believed in. Yeah. Opie was the only woman for him and with or without Nic's help, he was going to get her back.

He made a dash for the doorway separating the break room from the stairwell that led to Opie's apartment above the store. His hand turned the knob and everything in him went rigid—frozen. Like being stuck in Jell-o. No. Quicksand. Only, he wasn't sinking slowly into an abyss, he was rooted in limbo, unable to move. *Again. Shit.*

Hands grabbed at him, yanked him away from the door, and flung him to the ground. Nic stood over him, his chest heaving from the exertion. "We told you if you messed with Daphne you wouldn't be welcome here and we meant it."

Dax clamored to his feet and righted himself in time for Nic to send a fist flying into his face.

"Fuck!" He reared back from the impact. No way. He refused to let Nic walk away from this feeling superior. He bent at his waist and charged his brother, tackling him to the ground. The thunk of Nic's head meeting the floor spurred him on, and he landed blow after blow.

"All I wanted to do was help Opie. Why don't you understand?" Breathless, he stood and glared. "This is why Opie will never love you. You won't fight for her." Dax shook his head, turned for the door, and left.

FOUR

"ARE YOU OKAY?" Jason knelt beside Nic and offered him a hand.

"Yeah. Nothing I can't handle."

If the man was wounded anywhere besides his pride, Jason couldn't tell; his poker face remained intact.

"He's got one helluva temper," he hedged, hoping Nic could offer reassurances that his brother would cool off and then rejoin them in their mission to defeat Elech. With each person working together, they might be strong enough to take him down. Maybe.

"Yeah." Nic grabbed his hand and together they rose to their feet. "I've got to go and take care of something. Are you okay here with Daphne?"

"Of course. My spell seems to be holding and it will give me some time to find the Dewsberry spell book.

"Thanks, man. I'm not sure how I'd be able to help Callie without you."

"It's what I'm here for." He waited a beat then asked the question burning him from the inside out. "You love her, don't you?"

Nic stopped in his tracks but didn't turn around. "I've loved her from the first day we met, but I can see she doesn't love me back. I've lived in Dax's shadow waiting for her to notice me, and I'll wait in yours, but if she ever does decide she wants me, I'll be there waiting."

"Understood." It wasn't unexpected, but it still stung. What had he gotten himself into with Callie? Two men already fought for her affections and here he was thinking he could offer her something more. After this was over, he might need to reevaluate what the rest of his life should look like. He kept falling for unavailable witches. This one more so than the last between the twin suitors and the Jersey Devil.

Jason waited until he saw Nic drive away before he returned to the store to search for the spell book. A good witch would keep it close by, so here was as good a place to start as any. Besides, there wasn't a lot of time left to prepare for what he inevitably needed to do.

In the rear of the store, the books were older, as if they belonged to a private collection rather than a bookstore. Something in here had to be useful. *Right?* With a simple *Expose* spell, one of the books at the end of a shelf midway up a bookcase glowed with an eerie purple hue. A pentagram on the spine burst forth with lavender flames. He fingered the spine of the book and slid it from the shelf.

In his grasp, the book demanded, with an unnatural push, he walk toward the far corner of the store. There sat an armchair that looked old enough to be one his grandparents might've owned in the 1800's. The impulse to settle himself in the chair was impossible to ignore. He caressed the book's covers, eased it open, careful not to crack the aged spine, and inhaled the scent of Devil's Shoestring. The powerful herb was the book's own defense against evil. The darkness inside him faded deep down into the shadows of his being as the powdered herb entered his body on his inhalation.

Nice. Whoever had spelled this book had gone above and beyond to keep it well protected. A smile emerged on his face as he imagined a younger version of Callie's grandmother sitting with this very book in her lap, painstakingly dusting the powdered deterrent throughout the tome. In his vision, she shared Callie's blond locks and delicate features, but the influence of the devil was missing from her face.

Jason flipped the pages absently, not really sure what he searched for. About midway through the book, a flash of color from the corner caught his eye. He turned toward it, and seeing nothing, turned back to the book in his lap. The spell on the page in front of him was hastily scribbled in red ink with the only word recognizable being *"Passage."*

He ran an index finger over the letters and hoped they would arrange into readable words. When nothing happened, he sounded out the letters in their order on the page. The flash of color returned. The more he read, the brighter it became until a full-fledged transparent door appeared before him. Jason closed the book, tucked it beneath his arm, and moved closer to study it.

A tentative touch told him it was indeed real, solid, and not a figment of his imagination. The knob was cool in his hand as if it lived in a plane colder than the temperature-controlled store. In his grip, it turned without his moving and disappeared. He blinked and studied the now empty space. The moment of indecision he spent debating passed with a hurried heartbeat.

Crossing the threshold should've given him pause, but this wasn't the first time he'd stumbled upon something magically hidden. He shook a memory of his former flame's hidden torture chamber from his mind and continued forward. Unlike Teresa, who'd imprisoned him in her house of haunts, this room held the warmth only light magic exuded. There was nothing here to fear. The farther into the room he walked, the brighter the lights grew, dispelling the darkness and highlighting what looked very much like an apothecary. A long table sat in the middle of the room littered with neatly labeled vials, mortars holding various ingredients in different states of grounding, and pages of parchment with neatly scribed symbols and words.

There was no doubt about it—he'd crossed planes. It was one of those things he'd heard of as a young witch but never done. He toyed with the woodsy edge of a blank parchment. A bank of shelves lined the wall full of packages and bottles of herbs, tinctures, strange liquids— all ingredients

31

for spells. At the rear of the room stood two doors. They were nondescript in their appearance, nothing like the door he'd opened to gain admission into this room, but an unnatural sense emanating from them intrigued him. He approached the righter most of the two, but each step he took seemed to take him farther away. He halted after a dozen more steps. He was still no closer to the door, yet the table felt far enough away as if he'd walked half a city block. He turned toward the second door and reached for it.

The distance between his fingers and the second door closed with the speed of lightning in a summer sky, while the first door stood in the distance. The smooth solid pane of the second door collided with his fingertips. Etched in the dark wood was a symbol familiar to one he had known from a long time ago, yet different. The typical form of a pentagram but the circle surrounding the five peaks wasn't a circle at all. He ducked his head to get a closer peek at the design. A snake swallowing its own tail. An ouroboros. *Shit.* When the reality of what he saw collided with the dormant knowledge hidden deep within his memories, he took a hasty step back from the door. In the seconds it took for Jason to withdraw his hand from the wood, a cry sounded. Deep, insistent, commanding.

Whatever lay behind the door, he didn't want to know. The warning symbol said enough; enough to send him back to the table in the middle of the room to create the strongest potion he could remember.

He lit a small flame in a stone bowl, added the ingredients one at a time, and slid them around with a slender glass pipe until they melted together into a thick soup. He blew out the flame and poured a smidgen of rose water into the mixture. The cloying scent of ripe flowers tangled with the bitterness of the mashed Rowan berries and pulverized Dragon's blood. A column of twisting steam rose from the bowl, and Jason picked a small empty jar from the shelf behind him, holding it over the bowl, capturing the smoke as he slowly lowered the jar toward the mixture. He held it there until the liquid cooled and no more steam wafted upward. Once the steam cooled, it would regain a liquid form and be the most potent magic at his disposal. With quick hands, he tucked a cork into the mouth, sealing the contents inside.

He fumbled through a drawer tucked discretely into the underside of the table until he emerged with an inkwell, quill, and blank sticker-like labels. With a steady hand, he scratched the word *"Repel"* onto a section of sticker and tore it from its backing. When he was satisfied with the lack of bubbles in the smooth surface of the labeled jar, he dumped the remaining liquid into another jar and labeled it *"Revoke."* Without the essence of the superheated ingredients, this potion wasn't as strong as the original potion. All the dregs would do was give whoever ingested that version of the potion a slight stomachache when confronted with the object of their affection. It worked well when aiming to destroy a relationship of long standing. Lovers who literally couldn't stomach the sight of their mate tended to stray.

He smiled to himself and pocketed both jars. There was only enough of each for one dose, but it would be enough to achieve his plan. He needed Dax away from Daphne permanently to keep him from selling his sister to the devil, and he needed Nic to stop trying to vie for Callie's affections. Only when both brothers were incapacitated did he stand a chance at saving their sister and the woman he couldn't imagine living without.

A quick gander through the already bottled mixtures on the shelf revealed the owner of this place was a gifted witch with an abundant spell book at their disposal. He pocketed a small bottle of *Forget*, a mini bottle labeled *Command* with a bluish tint to the liquid inside and a folded paper packet with *Ignite* scrawled across the seal.

He plucked the book from the place he'd dropped it on the table and headed back toward the Dews, which flickered in his vision beyond the opening separating the planes. The return trip through the portal was more anticlimactic than his original trip had been. Jason toyed with the idea of replacing the book where he'd found it on the shelf, but a nagging sense of dread kept it firmly tucked beneath his arm.

"Where've you been? I've been looking for you for over an hour."

"Why aren't you upstairs?"

"I got bored. But I moved the chimes to the

back door, so we should still be okay." She chewed at the corner of her lip and flashed him a reticent look. "So, *where* were you for so long?"

Jason jumped when Daphne planted a hand on his shoulder. "Sorry. Time mustn't work the same way over there," he muttered dodging her grip.

"Over where? What are you talking about?"

Jason took a good gander at the woman and found the pallor of her skin pale and her eyes unfocused. "I'm sorry, Daphne. Don't worry. I have a plan. All I need is for you to stay here and wait until I come back for you."

Panic sprang to her face and her fingers crumbled the fabric of his shirt until her knuckles turned bright white under the stress of her death grip. "You can't leave me here alone. What if she comes back? What if Dax comes back? You heard him. He wanted to trade me for Callie."

He pried her hands off his shirt, tucked the book on an empty shelf, and enveloped her in a hug. "Shh, it's okay. I promise I won't let anything happen to you."

"Jason, please," she pleaded. "Don't go. Stay with me." She pressed her body into his, her softness soothing to the harsh reality of the moment, as his focus shifted gears.

"I have an idea." He pulled the bottle labeled *"Repel"* from his pocket and offered it to her. "Keep this. If anyone sets foot in this building looking for you, drink it. All of it. It'll taste like dirt, but it will keep you safe until I can get back here to you. Okay?" He folded her hand around the bottle and tilted her head up so her eyes were forced to meet his. "I need you to trust me, Daphne. Callie trusted me to care for you and you trust her, right?" When she nodded in the affirmative, he continued. "Then I need you to trust me on this. If anyone, and I mean anyone— your brothers, the devil, or even Callie—walk through that door, I need you to not even stop to think about it. Just open the jar and drink it all. Got it?" He stepped back and hoped she was strong enough to hold her own. She'd need to be. He needed to find the devil.

Daphne teetered but held strong. "If anyone comes here, I'll take the whole bottle," she promised, with only a trace of uncertainty in her voice.

"Good girl." He smiled to reinforce his praise. He watched as she tucked the bottle into the neckline of her shirt, leaving not a trace of it once she withdrew her hand. The woman sure had some tricks of her own up her sleeve, or in her brassiere, if he had to make a guess. She graced him with a small smile and headed back to the safety of the apartment upstairs from the shop. "I'll be back as soon as I can," he promised.

Now, all he had to do was not get himself killed.

FIVE

DRAMMELECH HATED BEING resigned to the shadows, but in small towns like Belvidere, it was best to not be seen often. Although, the shadows allowed him the ability to see what the humans tried so hard to hide.

They were crumbling. The pressure of keeping Daphne away from him was eating into their souls and making them question everything they believed.

Currently, his witch sat before him in the darkness, compelled to remove the shards of glass from his battered body while he considered his options. Of the three men within the bookstore, Dax was his most likely ally. He had already sought his counsel and made a deal. All he needed was something to push the man over the edge.

"Damn, witch! Careful," he scolded as a sharp shard was ripped from tender flesh of his face. She had done this to him and she would pay. He cracked his knuckles and flexed his fingers, anticipation soaring through his system.

Dax burst from the back door of the store, piss and vinegar running through his veins if his surly stance could be trusted. He pulled a phone from his pocket and dialed. Drammelech halted Calliope's ministrations with a curt wave of his hand and listened.

He was calling a woman. A woman who wasn't answering her phone. Interesting.

"Maureen, please, answer. Please?"

Ahh, this discovery would work to his advantage.

"Spell the motorcycle," he hissed at Calliope. "Make it break down a mile from here."

His compulsion held as the witch nodded and mumbled some words aimed at the Ducati in the parking lot. Now all he needed was the other Barren boy to get his plan underway.

Dax pocketed the phone and secured a helmet on his head before kicking over the engine on the bike while Drammelech debated sending Calliope back into the store to lure Nic out. If he sent the witch back in there was a chance his compulsion would waver as it had earlier. But if he waited and Nic didn't leave soon, he could miss the opportunity to convince Dax to join him.

He warred with himself for a moment while the tail light of the bike raced down the road. Like all good things brought with a little patience, Nic emerged from the store after Dax rounded a corner.

"Spell him to go to Maureen. Make him covet his brother's belongings. Make him stop at nothing to make her his. Nothing until he sets eyes on you. Then and only then will the compulsion end."

"No. Please, don't make me hurt them more."

Soft tears fell from her eyes and her body shook.

"You have little choice, witch. It's either you do as I ask, or I kill them all." He would never tire of seeing shock on the faces of those he coerced into commitments they couldn't escape. "Choose now."

The fall of her lashes was all he needed to see. She would do as he demanded and soon Dax would strike a bargain to bring Daphne to him.

His plan would succeed. He would rule this paltry plane soon enough and anyone who got in his path would be put down. Starting with the Barren family. Every last one of them. The Dewsberrys would be next on his hit list. And he mustn't forget the man who was working with them— Jason whoever he was. He and his family line would follow the rest into Hell for eternity.

SIX

"MAUREEN, ANSWER THE damn phone. I know you're there," Dax yelled into the receiver. *Shit.* He needed to see the woman and fast. He kicked the rear tire of his Streetfighter and cursed it for refusing to work. He knew this bike better than he knew himself and yet it's failure to run cut him to the core. He needed a release. He needed Maureen. He needed her now. He hung his helmet from the handlebar and started walking. She lived in town. Close enough that he could be there in under an hour if he kept a good pace.

It had only been a few days since he'd last graced her bed, but for some reason, tonight he couldn't imagine not sinking himself into her depths with reckless abandon, despite the battle being waged for his sister's soul, and the potential loss of Opie to the devil's right-hand-side. Nope.

None of that mattered in the least because the only thing resonating within him was desire. There was a hunger that begged to be fed, a need he owed to himself to fulfill despite the flicker of reason flashing in the dark corners of his mind.

The streets of Belvidere were quiet at night; the sounds of nature the only music to drown out his racing thoughts. He hated being without his bike. His boots sounded heavy with each step he took nearer to Maureen's little bungalow on the outskirts of town, away from the courthouse and park's downtown district. His feet were heavy, slow, unsure, and, try as he might, Dax couldn't shake the feeling of being stalked. Under every streetlamp, he paused and peered into the darkness, willing whatever lurked there to come into the light, but nothing came.

After walking the miles between his bike and her home, he rounded the last corner and was confronted by the truth of Maureen's avoidance. She had a guest. A dark truck sat in the drive and lights blazed behind curtained windows.

Dax glanced down at the glowing screen of his phone and ground his teeth together. It was almost midnight. There was no conceivable reason for *his* woman to entertain a guest this late and ignore his calls. The bite of possession shocked him. He'd never thought of Maureen as long term, but what she did in the bedroom made her worth keeping around.

He took the porch steps two at a time, the echo of his footfalls permeating the air. Yeah, if whoever was in there knew what was good for them, they'd pack it in and get the hell outta there. *Pronto.*

Dax went straight to the front door and tried the handle. The latch loosened under his hand as if guided to do so by unseen forces. The door swung inward and banged against the wall, a trumpet announcing his arrival. And it was, in a way. He belonged here, more than anyone else dared to believe. And it made him the only man who had rights to her treasures. The thought propelled him down the hallway leading to her bedroom. Noise from behind the door stopped him. He knew those sounds. Her whimpers, coos, and groans as she begged for more. Demanded her unseen lover to take her harder and higher, to a place where the thrill of passion hardened into a tangible thing. One she could reach out and touch before she slipped over the edge into the abyss of ecstasy. The sounds she should only make for him.

Shoulder to the door, Dax broke the wood at the hinges, unable to calm the rage boiling through his bloodstream.

"What the fuck are you doing?" His words bounced off every surface in the room. His lover stilled beneath the body of another man; a man who continued to pound his flesh into her without a shit to give about Dax.

Enraged, Dax stalked to the bed, ready to yank the man by the scruff of his neck, but a reflection in the mirror stopped him. Time stood still. The hum of a thousand swarming bees echoed in his ears as he rubbed away what his eyes demanded he see.

The man riding Maureen wasn't some stranger. Bile rose up in his throat and threatened to expunge itself in the middle of her floor. No. The man currently balls deep into his lover, taking her over the edge into bliss, was none other than his fucking brother.

Nic? *No.*

This wasn't happening. It couldn't be.

A scream ripped through the room, shattered the silence. Dax wondered where he'd gotten the breath to conjure such a noise, but it wasn't him. No. It was Maureen. She writhed against Nic as he fisted a hand in her hair, grounding them both as they took the plunge over the edge, uncaring about the show Dax witnessed. Uncaring about the ruination of all the relationships they'd had. Uncaring about the repercussions he would surely bring on them. He pounded a fist into the wall nearest to him and stalked from the room.

He couldn't watch any more. Couldn't stand to witness his brother's betrayal. Dax ran to the door, an escape from the pungent fumes of their treachery, from the sound of their bliss, from them, from himself. He ran until his boots hit the sidewalk in front of Maureen's house, and he ensnared himself in the awkward embrace of his enemy.

"Let'ssss make a deal," the devil hissed, his forked tongue dancing in the night air. "Your sssissster for your brother." A wicked smile crept across his face and a single eyebrow rose nearly into his hairline.

The image of Nic in the throes of pleasure tore at him and another ecstatic scream punctured the night, plunging his heart into further disrepair. "Yes. I'll take the deal." He offered the devil his hand as a familiar blond head darted beneath a streetlamp.

"No."

Opie's voice was downright magical. It never ceased to amaze him how beautiful even a single word could sound as it poured from her lips. She raced across the street toward him as if her sole purpose in life was to drive him from the ledge. He blinked once, twice, and felt the icy cold grip of Elech's hand in his as Callie bounded into him.

"Dammit, Dax. What've you done?"

Her words held meaning, but he no longer cared. Everything that made him feel anything dissolved. He reveled in the emptiness.

Content to feel nothing.

SEVEN

JASON LOVED PARLOR tricks. Many moons ago, before Teresa had cursed him into the window, they had been his specialty. And the trail of blinking fireflies he followed through the town was one of his favorites. A simple spell aimed at tracking someone appeared impressive to anyone who wasn't schooled in the craft. He rounded the corner onto Second Street and stopped dead in his tracks. On the sidewalk stood Dax and the devil, hands clasped.

No. The idiot hadn't been desperate enough to make a deal with the devil, had he? No. There was no way Dax would do that to Callie. Daphne, sure, but not Callie. She appeared as if his thoughts had conjured her. Hair flying wild, Callie sprinted across the empty street, a cry ripped from the core of her.

The ruckus was loud enough to spark lights in nearby windows and start a symphony of well-meaning pets-turned-guard-dogs in the dark.

From the front door emerged an underwear-only-clad Nic, followed by a pretty woman in a robe. The woman yelled at Dax and Nic threw out an arm to hold her back.

Jason ducked into the shadows and moved ever closer to the scene being played out on the front lawn. Tears streamed down Callie's face, the other woman hurled insults toward Dax, and the devil laughed a full belly laugh as he turned to face Nic.

"Your loyal brother has offered you up as a trade," he taunted. "He'll deliver your sister to me, and I'll deliver your corpse to him."

Even from a yard away, Jason could make out a twinkle of joy in the devil's eye. *Impossible.* This was going to hell in a flaming handbasket of doom faster than Jason could track. If the devil killed Nic, there wasn't anyone to stand beside him in defense of Daphne. Callie and Dax had agreements to adhere to now, and Jason didn't doubt for a second their unimportance, once the devil had what he wanted.

It was stupid, he reasoned with himself, to care so much for people who were practically strangers to him. But this was his chance at a do-over in life. Now was the time to be better than his former self had, and do the right thing. For once.

Selflessness wasn't his typical state of being, and it felt heavy in his heart as he stepped from the shadows. "Don't you think you've done enough damage already, Devil?"

The woman on the porch stopped yelling and cowered behind Nic as the ground beneath their feet began to tremble.

"Witch, haven't you learned yet? I'll kill her before you can stop me. I've seen your best tricks, and I'm ready for them this time."

The gusto that ran through his bloodstream curdled into a bone-deep chill as the devil turned his focused attention on him. If there was any part of Callie still accessible, this was her cue to jump into the mix. When he met her eyes around the imposing breadth of the devil's shoulders, Jason worried he'd misjudged her. The tears in her eyes flowed freely down her cheeks, splashing on her shirt, undeterred.

Damn. He was in trouble.

"You can have her," he declared, false bravado unwavering in his voice. "She chose you over me anyway. And so did her dumb-ass lover. You can have them both for all I care." He hated how harsh the words sounded in the quiet. Regret sank through him with the speed of molten lava when Callie dropped her eyes to the street.

"See, asshole, I knew you were still fucking her," yelled the woman on the porch, presumably at Dax. "Serves you right to find your brother in my bed."

"Get inside, Maureen," Nic commanded. "Stay out of this."

The ground shook once more beneath them as the woman on the porch's temper rose. What she was, Jason had no idea, but he would bet she was definitely not all human.

"Don't talk to her like that," Dax hollered at his brother. He broke free from his spot on the sidewalk and raced toward the front porch and Nic.

"Stop," Callie cried, hands flying into the air on instinct, a spell bristling beneath her big blue eyes.

It was now or never. Jason reached into his pocket, pulled the packet of *Ignite* from his pocket, and ripped through the paper with his teeth. As the powdered substance kicked up in the air, he held his breath, unsure of what it would do. At the same time, Callie sent a rippled current through the air. It knocked Dax to the ground, pushed Maureen into the doorjamb, and pulled Nic's feet out from beneath him. The devil screeched, and Jason ducked as the pulse of her power assaulted them. Flecks of powder landed on Dax and a grunt became the baseline to the devil's tenor in a harmony of agony.

Jason peered up at the devil. He flailed, patting at bits of heat landing on his elegant suit before he turned on Callie, grabbed her by the hair, and pulled a blade from the inside of his suit jacket.

"Stop. All of you," he hissed. Curls of smoke wafted up from his body, but he no longer seemed bothered by the heat permeating through to his skin beneath his clothes, unlike Dax, who still rolled in the grass fighting the flames. "I'm tired of wasting my time with you. Bring me what I demand, and I'll spare whoever delivers her." He pressed the tip of the blade to Callie's throat and turned a menacing glare on Jason. "In case you needed to be properly motivated, witch, it's only one of you that will walk away tonight." He arched an eyebrow. "It can be her if you bring me the other one." A downright playful smile crept across his face.

"No," Callie whimpered.

A roll of emotions washed over her and he knew this wasn't going to end well.

Dax staggered to his feet and smoothed his jacket. "We made a deal. I'll bring her to you."

The words left his mouth and Callie made her move. With closed eyes, she grabbed the hilt of the dagger, kicked at the devil's shins, and when he relinquished his grip on the weapon, she yanked it free and threw it through the air, aimed swift and surely at Dax's chest.

Not a sound was heard as the blade sank into the flesh hidden beneath the fabric of his shirt. Not even from Dax. Instead, his face creased in confusion as he stared at Callie, uncertainty the only emotion on his face.

"I'm sorry."

Her apology fell short of Dax's comprehension as his knees hit the ground and his coloring went ashen in the moonlight. And then the screams started.

EIGHT

BEDLAM BROKE OUT everywhere Jason's eyes fell.
Everywhere.

Thirteen wasted no time in pulling the dagger
from Dax's dying body before he disappeared.
Maureen's screams echoed in the night, agitated
the ground beneath them, and called many an
onlooker from the comfort of their bed. Callie fell to
the ground at Dax's side and pressed her hands
hard on the deep wound while Nic worked to quiet
a distraught Maureen. Jason's eyes swiveled
between Callie and Nic. *Ugh.*

Why did every decision have to end with
disappointing her? The one who needed him most
was Nic. The hysteric woman on the porch would
be trouble for all of them. A quick once-over of
Dax's dying body sent a surge of relief through his
bloodstream. Decision made. He sidestepped Callie

and Dax and made his way to Nic's side.

"Give this to her. It'll calm her down," he said and offered Nic the bottle of *Forget* from his pocket.

"What is it?" Nic studied the bottle in his hand, brow creased, while Jason smoothed a hand through Maureen's hair.

"I need you to trust me on this…" Jason paused and inclined his head toward the hysterical woman. "It will calm her and make this night a thing of the past."

"Gotcha." Nic pocketed the vial, gathered the woman into his arms, and carried her into the house.

Before Jason could decide how best to handle Callie and Dax, a neighbor called from their front porch to say they had called for an ambulance and the police.

Dread settled in the pit of his stomach. The authorities would not understand what had happened here. Not even with a damn crystal ball at their disposal. Instead of going to Callie, Jason crossed the threshold and followed the sounds of the woman's tears.

"Here, babe. Drink this. It'll help." He heard Nic soothe.

"I can't. I just need… I shouldn't have let you come in. Dax would still be alive," she sobbed, her words a garbled mess of clipped phrases and cries. "That awful bitch was jealous of me from day one," she said, her cries broken by hiccups.

Jason stood outside the bedroom and listened. Whatever had happened before he'd arrived was a

51

mystery, and, therefore, he couldn't fathom why Callie would be the one to send the dagger straight into Dax's chest.

"It's my fault. I don't know what came over me tonight," Nic said. "It's like all of a sudden, I wanted to do something to hurt him, and next thing I knew, here I was."

"Wait. So you didn't come here for me? You bastard. You. Lied. To. Me."

The sounds of skin striking skin sent Jason into motion again. He rounded the corner into the open doorway. "Hey. Is everything okay in here?"

"Yeah. Everything's fine," Nic answered, as the woman glared at him from the bed. The red handprint on his face was the only indicator of his deceit. Nic rose from the bed and plucked the vial of *Forget* off the nightstand. "Take this, Maureen. It really will help." He held it out to her and she shrank away as if it might bite.

Jason stepped into the room, took the vial from Nic's outstretched hand, and sat beside Maureen. "Nic, can you go outside with Callie and help her until the authorities arrive? I'll stay here and keep an eye on Maureen." He waited until Nic nodded and then turned back to the blond in the bed. "Darling, you've had one hell of a night. Let me help take care of you."

"I can't believe I let that asshole into my house and my bed. I should've known he didn't really want me. You know him and Dax, always fight over things. Dax has said from day one that whatever he wanted, Nic had to have. No wonder he was here. But after everything with Dax, I thought maybe it was a fresh start. A guy who didn't cheat with his ex when the going got tough. Silly me to think he was here to do the stand-up thing that Dax couldn't do." She dropped her head into her hands and cried. "Now who's going to help me raise this kid?"

The words came out soft and were coated in tears, but were as unmistakable as an angel in the Underworld. Oh, shit. This woman was in deeper than he could get her out of.

"Let me get you a glass of water, honey," Jason soothed. "It'll help wash away the tears." He pocketed the bottle of *Forget* as he left the room. There was no way in hell he was going to let Callie or Nic know Dax had fathered a kid. Besides, if the secret died with Dax, then there was a chance the devil would never find out either.

He opened cabinet doors in her kitchen until he found the glasses, plucked one from a paper-lined shelf, and turned on the spigot. He let the water run until cool and then poured the *Forget* into the glass. He didn't dare add water in case it would reduce the potion's potency. Jason returned to the room, handed her the glass and waited until the contents went down in one large gulp.

"You mustn't've let the water run long enough. It tasted metallic. Happens sometimes with these old houses." She held out the glass with a wrinkle on her face.

"I'll get you some more," he offered, taking the offered glass.

"It's all right. I think I'm going to lie down for a few minutes. I'm sure I'll need to talk to the police when they arrive."

He helped tuck the covers around her and gave a gentle pat on the head. Before he left the room with the glass, her breathing had shifted into the pattern of deep sleep. Good. It was what she needed to let the events of this evening melt away.

He rounded the corner from the kitchen and ran smack into the detective from the other day.

"If you're in here, that can't mean anything good for the guy out there," Jason quipped and stepped back from the man who could overshadow a shed with his height.

"Sorry to be the bearer of bad news," the man quipped in way of agreement.

"Not all bad news is bad," Jason retorted. "Charlie, right?" He offered his hand.

"Yeah. I never really got how you played into things earlier, and now I find you here with another dead body." Charlie scrutinized him with the authority of a well-seasoned detective.

Charlie had been the first on the scene at Daphne's B & B when the devil had attacked today, no, it was finally yesterday. Maybe it would mean today would be the day Jason could regain some control over the situation at hand and do what needed to be done to save both Daphne and Callie. He glanced at his beloved pocket watch and hoped it could be true.

Charlie cleared his throat, pulling Jason back from his thoughts. He couldn't be that bad of a guy. After all, he'd been the one to let them go and help cover up their involvement in the devil's murder of Lisa Dewsberry, aka Callie's Grams.

The scent of sandalwood hung in the air between them, comforting, soothing, enticing. He assessed Charlie and found him worthy.

"If I told you I was freed from a cursed window after sixty-nine years yesterday morning, would you believe me?" he asked. Cheeky as it sounded, the truth was unbelievable even to his ears. "And if I said I was here following a really bad guy who had threatened Calliope Dewsberry, the same man who killed Lisa Dewsberry, would you believe that?"

"You'd be surprised what I'd believe these days." Charlie scratched at the stubble on his chin and avoided direct eye contact. "So, I was told Maureen saw everything. Where is she?"

Yeah, this guy had some secrets of his own, Jason decided. "Ah, she just fell asleep. Can it wait until later?" He needed to give the potion time to fully work.

"For now. But, I'll need someone to wake her soon. Did you happen to see it go down?"

"I did. But it might be one of those things you'd have to see to believe." Jason shrugged his shoulders when Charlie eyed him, suspicion lingering in the air separating them. "The devil did it. He used a dagger and killed Dax when he refused to turn over Daphne Barren."

"The victim's sister?"

"Yup. Callie almost got killed in the struggle,

and the ruckus woke poor Nic and Maureen up," Jason added for good measure.

"Is there more to this that I should 'unofficially' know?" Charlie sent a measured look Jason's way. "Something that could land you or Callie in trouble?"

"Daphne Barren is going to need protection, but not the kind the authorities can give. I have certain skills which will help, but I don't think it's going to be enough." Jason raised a brow and wiggled his fingers. "As far as Maureen is concerned, I don't think she'll remember much about tonight when she wakes, but she'll need some help when she learns Dax is dead. Turns out, they were together a while back before she and Nic started seeing one another." Jason gave an exaggerated wink. "But Calliope's going to need some help, too. The devil has her under control or something. I can't get a grip on it to undo it, which means she'll need someone watching out for her if things keep going badly and she's in the vicinity when they occur—if you get my meaning."

Charlie waited a beat, and in the time it took for him to respond, Jason wondered if he'd made a huge mistake in trusting this man.

"I have a friend who can help keep an eye on Daphne," he offered. "He has some unique talents as well."

"Like the woman you sent to help Callie out of the pond?" Jason asked, an eyebrow raised.

"Like her," Charlie agreed. "Colin is as trustworthy as they come, and if there's anything he can do to protect Daphne, he will. As far as Callie's concerned, I'll do what I can to keep her out of as much trouble as possible, but you need to keep being up front with me. I can't do my job and convince the humans everything is normal if I'm not in on the whole story. Got it?"

"Agreed. Some day you and I are going to have to sit down and discuss this 'us' versus 'them' thing you have going on," Jason chided. "Far as I can tell, you're still human."

"Not everything that appears human is human," Charlie rebutted.

"Eh, I disagree. You can be part 'other' and part human, and still be recognized as human. I've had years to contemplate all sides of this argument. Trust me." Jason offered his hand to Charlie. "Thanks for looking out for her. I'll owe you one if she makes it out of this fiasco alive."

"No problem. Us 'others' need to stick together," Charlie agreed, taking Jason's hand. "Where can I tell Colin to meet you?"

"The Daily Dews. But if he can't make it in the door, he's out," Jason warned.

"What?"

"He'll understand when he gets there." Jason rolled his shoulders, squared them, and walked past Charlie toward the front door.

"Where are you going?" Charlie called after him.

"I'm free to go. Aren't I, officer?" Jason muttered a compulsion spell under his breath and continued his path to the door.

"Oh. Yeah. Just don't leave town," Charlie called after him.

"Wouldn't dream of it," he muttered.

"But Dominic Barren is staying put," Charlie added.

What is it about cops always having the last word? Jason shook his head but didn't turn back.

NINE

JASON WASTED NO time rearranging the bells on both entryways leading into the Dews. It was easy for Charlie to say Colin was a good guy, but until he passed the first test, there was no telling whether he would be under the influence of the devil. Daphne stared at the front door from a safe distance, while he paced, waiting.

"Callie'll be pissed if you wear out the floorboards," Daphne called from a seat at one of the reading tables near the back of the store.

"She'll be even more upset if I let some stranger walk in here and take you away," he rebutted. "Do you know this guy Colin?" Jason paused his round-trip as the noise of a car on the street sent his nerves into overdrive.

"Not sure. If he's been in here before, I might recognize him, but I don't remember a Colin from school."

Jason waved at her to hush as the car drew closer and slowed to a stop in front of the building. "I think we're about to meet him," he said and ducked behind the counter as if the store was open and ready for business. Never mind that it was still the middle of the night, it couldn't be more than four a.m., one of the display windows was shattered, and the owner had lost her mind and potentially her soul to the damn devil. Jason shook the last thought from his head and leaned on his elbows, as a man the size of a human icebox ambled up to the door. "Shit." Jason whistled under his breath. "Sure you don't know him," he whisper-yelled to Daphne.

Her mouth was gaping, chin making its way to the floor, and her eyes were wide, as she stared at the man in the doorway.

"Huhlo?" he called into the store without even attempting to cross the threshold.

"Hi. You Colin?" Jason called from behind the counter, also not making a step toward the doorway.

"Yup. Charlie called and asked me to stop by. Said some guy needed help keeping an eye on some girl. You that guy?" He rubbed a hand over his barely-there brown hair and waited.

"I'm Jason. Why don't you come on in?" He called, his breath caught in his throat.

"Charlie said something about minding the door." He gave a tentative push on the handle to see if it would move. "Is it safe?"

"Sure is…" Jason nodded, "as long as you aren't planning on doing something regretful."

Colin nodded as if the warning made all the sense in the world and opened the door fully. "So, what can I do to help?" he asked, once the door closed behind him.

Jason turned toward Daphne and bit back a laugh. She still sat staring in open-mouthed wonder at Colin. "Have you met Daphne Barren before?" He waved a hand in her direction. "She's who we're keeping an eye on. There's a devil after her," he added, waiting for Colin's reaction.

"The Jersey Devil?" he questioned. "I thought he was only a legend."

"Not a legend. A real-life-pain-in-the-ass." From the corner of his eye, he saw Daphne move. He shook his head. "Turns out she's related to him in a long-lost kind of way, and he thinks he needs her to open the gates of Hell or something."

Colin nodded and Jason was impressed with his lack of surprise.

"What are you?" Daphne's awe-laced question surprised them both. "I mean, you're built like a linebacker, but there's something about you that screams 'other'." She made her way across the room, head tilted and eyes crinkled at the corners as she studied him.

"I'm the same as you," Colin answered carefully enough that it piqued Jason's interest.

"I doubt that," Jason argued. "She's related to a devil, I'm a witch…" he paused to give the other man the once over, "and there's no way in hell either of those things apply to you."

"You got me there," Colin answered without further explanation. "So, what's the plan here? I've never actually seen a devil, so I sure don't have an idea how to protect someone from one."

"Well, I've managed to get lucky so far, when I've gone up against him, but Callie had some help at the B & B." He turned to Daphne. "Who was it she said took over her body again?"

Colin blanched and Daphne looked thoughtful for a moment. "Delila someone I think. Yeah, that sounds about right. Delila. The ancestor who started this whole mess." As she gained confidence in her answer, her voice grew louder. "That's who we need. Delila."

"Wait a minute. Someone took over someone else's body?" Confusion clouded Colin's face.

"Witches be tripping," Jason intoned, using vernacular he'd heard from kids on the street while stuck in his window. "Although, even if I'm able to commune with her, I'm not sure it will do us any good."

"We have to try." Daphne grabbed his arm and graced him with the most pathetic puppy eyes he'd ever witnessed in all his years. "Please, Jay. Don't let Thirteen keep hurting my family. Please."

Guilt bubbled and burned in his gut. He stuffed the truth about Dax into the depth of his soul and gave her a reassuring pat on the arm. "I'll try, but there's no telling if she will even respond if I can contact her. Plus, we don't have Callie to act as the medium this time, so it might not even work."

"What's a medium?" Colin moved closer to them and lowered his voice after making a barely conspicuous look over his shoulder. "Where's this Delila person hiding?"

Jason threw his hands up in surrender. "I don't know where she is. She's a ghost for God's sake. She could be anywhere. And without a connection to her, I'm not sure how we can contact her. An old school séance would be the most practical way, but there's no guarantee it'll work."

Daphne's grip on his arm tightened. "We do have a connection to her."

"No, we don't. We can't trust Callie right now. The devil has her under his control," Jason reminded her.

"Not Callie. Me." The words hung heavy in the space between them, pregnant with the truth of her lineage.

"You're not a witch. I'm not sure you could withstand it if she possessed you." Jason stared at the woman he'd sworn to protect and weighed the options.

A tug on his arm and more of those damned puppy eyes and he was actually considering her harebrained idea. How bad could it be? A simple séance. Maybe Delila answered, maybe she didn't. Worst case, there would be a little body snatching. It wouldn't last long if it went anything like when Callie was possessed. He swiveled between the woman clutching his arm and the muscle sent to help protect her. Yeah, they were running out of options, and fast.

"Okay. We can try it." Jason contemplated what he'd need. If at all possible, he wanted to stay clear of the room on the other plane. "We can't do it here, though. And we'll need some supplies."

He rattled off a list and Daphne went to work gathering what he needed. Colin hung a tarp over the broken window and hung a sign on the door. Soon it would be daybreak and the regulars would otherwise file in, desperate for a cup of joe. When they had everything gathered, Daphne showed them upstairs into Callie's apartment.

"I'm sure she won't mind us using her place. As long as we don't use up all her coffee, she'll never need to know." A tight smile pinched Daphne's face as she set the candles and piece of parchment she'd been carrying down with a sigh.

"You must really care for your friend, if you're willing to go through all this for her," Colin said, gesturing at the items sprawled on the dining room table.

Daphne nodded. "It's nothing she wouldn't do for me."

"You mean she hasn't already done for you," Jason announced, setting up the candles. "She was possessed yesterday to save your hide. She lost her grandmother saving your ass. She even killed her old lover when the idiot made a damn deal with the devil to hand you over in exchange for Nic's death…" The words spilled out unbidden, and the abject silence was the only thing that stopped Jason from continuing on.

"What did you say?" Daphne's hand shook, the

lighter she'd found in the kitchen threatening to slip through her fingers and clatter to the floor. "What did my brothers do?"

"Dammit," Jason muttered. "I didn't want to tell you until we had a solution."

"Is Dax dead? Yes or no?" There was no bravado or laughter, or even confusion in her voice. Stark acceptance was all she had to offer with her question.

Jason didn't have the heart to worsen the blow with words, so he nodded the affirmation she needed.

"How?"

"I think the devil has the dagger Callie needed. He was threatening to kill Callie with it, and she was able to get it away from him..." he trailed off.

Daphne listed to the right, her legs no longer able to hold her. Colin wrapped her in his thick arms and effortlessly carried her to the couch. Rather than set her down alone, he dropped himself into the cushions, bracing her descent with his body. He cradled her to his chest and stroked her hair as silent tears dripped down her cheeks.

"I'm sorry, Daphne. I really am. Callie had no choice. Dax was upset. He made a horrible decision. The only way for Callie to help him was to break the contract. Killing him before he could get to you was the only way." His explanation sounded like excuses, even to his own ears, and he hated the effect his words had on the woman who looked so small and fragile in Colin's arms. "You have to understand, she did it for you."

A small nod was all he got in return for his efforts.

TEN

ONCE DAPHNE CALMED down, Jason got everything ready for the séance. It had been decades since he'd last performed one, but luckily for him, Teresa had used them as a moneymaking side job well into her old age. Most people thought she was a quack fortuneteller, but he could attest to her fine skills in the art of communing with the dead.

He purposefully placed six candles, three white, three black, in the center of the table around a small dish filled with jellybeans they found in one of the kitchen drawers. The scent of lavender incense mixed with the scent of sandalwood, as he sparked a flame at the end of the incense stick. As the dark energy swirled in him, fighting for a way out, he unwrapped a piece of devil's shoestring, placed it on a dish, and touched the flame from the lighter to it. The dried root caught flame and began to burn. Might as well cover all angles and ward off the evil entities his dark essence was liable to attract before bothering to open the conduit.

"It smells like something died in here," Daphne complained as she and Colin walked to the table hand in hand.

"It's supposed to," Jason replied and gestured for each of them to take a seat. "Now, here's the plan. We all hold hands and I start chanting. Once she makes contact, I will ask her to give us a sign by making a noise. If she's as strong as she seemed yesterday, there's a good chance she'll be able to. I'll ask her to try stepping into your body, Daphne, and she'll likely require you to verbally offer her your submission. If that happens, all you have to do is invite her to share your consciousness for a short time." He sat at the head of the table and reached both hands out toward Daphne and Colin. "If anything else comes through, I'll let go of your hands. If I let go, you both let go, too. Anything still connecting the circle is the same as giving permission to a spirit to linger. So, let me say it again, if I let go, you both let go, too. Understand?"

"Sure," Colin nodded. "Nothing like inviting a demon to the party. The devil's already here, right?"

"Not exactly," Daphne corrected. "He's a devil, but not *the* devil."

Jason rolled his eyes and picked up the blank piece of parchment. With a pen he'd found in Callie's kitchen, he scrawled Delila in big bold letters.

"Okay, let's get started." He wrapped his hand around Daphne's and flashed Colin a caustic stare before doing the same to his. "Spirits on this plane, one amongst you is needed. Delila, please come forward." He paused a beat and repeated the invocation again. "Spirits on this plane, one amongst you is needed. Delila, please come forward." The flame on the white candle nearest to him flickered low, as if it was about to go out, then blazed brighter than all the remaining five put together. "I think we have Delila," he whispered to Daphne and Colin. "Delila, if you are with us, please knock once."

All three around the table held their collective breath and listened. A swift rap sounded from behind Daphne and she and Colin jumped. A smile crossed Jason's face. "Glad you could join us, Delila. Calliope needs your help. She's the witch you helped before and she needs you again. The devil has coerced her into making a deal."

The fire crackled and Jason felt a push at the center of his being. Delila was trying to communicate with him.

"The woman at this table has offered her body for your use this morning. She willingly gives that of herself, so we can stop the devil."

A chill ran down the arm extended toward Daphne. A quick glance at her confirmed his suspicion that the chill had continued up her arm. Her eyes were wide and darted between his and Colin's. Her mouth fell open, wordless, and her stare went blank. The black candles on the table flickered and extinguished on their own, leaving only the soft glow of the white candles remaining.

"Who are you who summons me, witch?"

It was Daphne's voice, but the intonation was all wrong.

"Delila? Is that you?"

"You're wasting my time. My son has horrible plans for this child and needs to be stopped."

"Your son?"

"Drammelech is my son. Your Calliope knew it to be true. But he's too strong to be stopped alone."

"That's why we called you here. We were hoping you could help us. Daphne can lend you her body and I can lend you my power. Together, it might be enough to stop him."

"Silly witch. Even with all our powers combined, we cannot stop Elech. He's half-witch himself. We are lacking the devil half of the equation."

"The *devil*, devil?" Colin's voice sounded foreign compared to Daphne's.

"Demogorgon," Daphne answered, and a wry smile creased her lips. "Ah, I've missed the sound of his name on my tongue." Daphne smiled wider. "Dema," she purred.

"How do we reach Dema?" Jason asked, concern gripping his heart as he watched Daphne slowly morph into a character unlike herself.

"Ah…" Daphne hummed. "We'll have to undo the spell."

"What spell?" Colin asked, his grip tightening on Jason's hand.

"The one that locked the bastard in Hell."

After Daphne recited the needed ingredients for completing the spell, Jason thanked Delila and released Daphne's hand. He followed suit with Colin and waited for Colin and Daphne to do the same. Instead, Daphne glared at Jason and snickered.

"Did you think this would be it? Come on, witch, you had to know that I would want to stay and assist." Daphne's head cocked at an odd angle and her knuckles turned white as they gripped Colin's hand harder.

Panic flashed over Colin's face as he struggled to free himself from the grip without hurting the woman clinging to him.

"It isn't Daphne," Jason urged. "Do whatever you need to do to break the circle," he demanded. "Break her damn hand if it comes to it."

Daphne's eyes went wide, then narrowed. "You wouldn't hurt me though, would you, Colin?" She dipped her lashes over her brilliant blue eyes and peered at him through them. "You like me too much to hurt me. Don't you?" She paused a beat, then continued. "I can tell you've been hurt before. Someone you cared for disappointed you. Didn't she? And now, here you are, looking for love in another place it can never be." Daphne tsk-tsked and used her other hand to caress a trail up his arm with her index finger. "This body belongs to another as long as I inhabit it. And once I'm done, I'm not sure you'll want it." She blinked and turned toward Jason. "Daphne's accepted her destiny. I think you need to accept yours." With that, Daphne released Colin's hand and rose to her feet.

"Get what we need. Dema's waited long enough," she called behind her as she left Callie's apartment and the stunned men in her wake.

ELEVEN

"WHAT JUST HAPPENED?" Colin cradled his hands in his lap and refused to move from his seat. "You said once the circle broke, Delila would leave. Only, I'm not convinced she didn't walk outta here with Daphne's body." Colin's tone was low and Jason had to inch closer to hear him. "And what's this stuff about Dema? Is he a devil, too?"

"I think he might be *the* devil." Jason blew out the remaining candles and cleared off the table. "Not so sure this was a good idea after all."

"You think? Delila is walking around in Daphne's body and wants us to break the devil out of Hell. Nothing about any of that is good." Colin stood and cracked the knuckles in his hands. "So now what?"

"Now you keep an eye on Delila, but don't let on you know it's her, and I'll put together the potion she asked for. I know where to find the bones she requested, but I'll need a ride to get them."

"Sure. I'll babysit the body snatcher, and then be your chauffeur." Colin rolled his eyes and headed for the apartment door. "Don't take long, man. I'm not sure how convincing I can be."

"Be convincing enough to keep her here, because I don't want her taking off without us." They exchanged a meaningful head nod. "I'll be as quick as I can, but the place where I can find the ingredients doesn't work on the same time as here does." Colin shot him a strange look. "Don't ask. I'm still not sure how it works, but I'll be able to get everything she needs."

Jason tucked the book of shadows he'd found earlier under his arm, clomped down the stairs, and went straight into the back reading area. Before cracking the spine, he gave a cursory glance to make sure Daphne/Delila wasn't anywhere within earshot. Convinced he was alone, he opened the book and recited the incantation for *Passage*. As it had before, a door appeared, beckoning him back into the sanctuary the old apothecary room offered. Once he'd crossed the threshold, the Dews disappeared behind him.

A lone stool sat tucked beneath the solitary table in the room. Without too much thought on the fact the stool hadn't been there before, he kicked it out and perched on it, wracking his brain for a spell—any spell—as long as it would put everything right. Forget what Delila said she required to deal with the devil, he needed to ensure Delila couldn't permanently share Daphne's body—because, with his luck, she'd do whatever it took to take down the devil, including kill Callie.

He put the book on the table and cradled his head in his hands under the pressure. One spell. All he needed was one spell to turn everything around. A noise pulled him from his thoughts. The book, previously closed, was now open and flipped through itself as if unseen fingers were at work. When it paused on a page long enough for him to read, the word *'Reveal'* seeped into existence from the ether. He scanned the page, noting the ingredients he'd seen before in the room and scribbling the ones he hadn't down on a piece of parchment, in case the fickle book decided to mask the spell once more.

It only seemed to take a few minutes to find the ingredients and return to the table, but Jason worried how long it had been since he left Colin and Daphne alone. He took a deep breath, centered his intentions on the revealing power his brewing potion would have, and plucked a clean jar from the shelf. The potion smelled nothing like anything he'd ever brewed before. Whether it was the heady scent of the star anise or the dried flakes labeled Purpurescens, he wasn't sure. But the heated mixture wafted a licorice scent that wrinkled his nose. If he needed to get someone to ingest this potion, he was sunk. There was no way anyone with a working set of nostrils would willingly put this in their body. He poured the liquid into the jar and capped it, grateful the odor dissipated soon after the liquid was sealed away.

One task complete, Jason set the jar aside and gathered the list of ingredients Delila had requested. He closed the book, tucked it into the back of his trousers, and filled his hands with the menagerie of jars, packets, and bottles on the table. When he went to pick up the jar of *Reveal*, it no longer held the dark coloring it had been when he'd poured it into the jar. Now it appeared as clear as water. He twisted off the cap and gave it a sniff. Huh. Innocuous as water. Impressive. Whatever energy had recommended the spell, hadn't steered him wrong. He secured the lid and slid this jar into his trouser pocket. He didn't need Delila getting wind of what he was thinking. Not if he wanted her help to deal with the devil. Or devils, to be more precise, if Dema joined the party.

Jason stepped through the magical doorway leading back into the Dews with trepidation in his wake. He didn't want to give away the location of this secret space to Delila, but he didn't know how much longer Colin could keep her in the dark. It wouldn't take much for her to figure out they were on to her. Crossing the threshold was anticlimactic and gave his nerves a much-needed rest. He walked into the break room area behind the curtain and found Colin sitting at the table with Daphne. Both nursed cups of coffee, and she was engrossed in the morning paper.

"Find what you needed?" Colin asked with an eyebrow raised.

"Sure did. You ready to head out to the farm?"

"The farm?" Daphne's eyes lit, her nostrils flared, and betrayed Delila hidden beneath Daphne's exterior.

"That's where the bones are. We buried them under a tree overlooking the old family plot."

"When?" She narrowed her eyes, pinning him to his spot on the floor.

"Yesterday, when Callie almost got eaten by the pond." Jason cocked his head and stroked his chin, challenge in his glare. "Don't you remember?"

Daphne rose from her seat and shrugged. "Oh, those bones. I thought you said we needed Delila's bones."

"They are her bones. They're why the lake almost killed Callie. She spelled it to kill any of her relatives willing to go in there to retrieve the bones. She never wanted the spell undone." This back and forth without showing his hand was getting tedious. "I'm pretty sure she was willing to sacrifice you to get them out," he accused, pointing a finger at Daphne.

"What? How?"

"You're an ancestor, too, you know. Even if it comes by way of her son."

Daphne/Delila stood there in open-mouthed silence. She hadn't thought it through. He could tell by the visible "oh shit" etched on her face. Getting those bones using Daphne's body would've sent her back to her ghostly state. Yeah, he had her now.

"Ready?" He directed the question at Colin and headed toward the door.

"You betcha."

*****

Watching a witch as powerful as Delila in action was a rare treat. They stood beside the freshly packed earth hiding her bones and waited for them to appear under her command. Standing on her land, Delila no longer bothered to maintain her Daphne facade. Instead, she moved about as if she still owned the land and everything buried beneath it.

Jason stepped back when the soil at his feet trembled.

"Shit. What's that?" Colin asked, pointing at peaks of gold springing forth from the freshly moved soil like daffodils in the spring.

"My bones."

Delila's words were an awed whisper wrapped in Daphne's voice and chilled Jason to the bone. "How are you still here, walking among us?"

"She allows it." The answer sounded so simple. As each bone pierced the surface, she lovingly plucked it from the ground like a newly opened bud. "We need a flat surface to lay them out."

"How 'bout one of those graves over there. They appear pretty level," Colin suggested, pointing into the old family plot as the sun splintered the horizon and made its way into the sky.

"I think that should do," Jason agreed, heading toward the stone markers.

"It needs to be a place of significance," Daphne's voice rang out behind him. "A place where earth magic would mingle with my own."

"Like the place your tombstone is?" Colin asked as he cleared the brush beside a stone.

"No. My body was never interred there, so it would have no magic within it." Daphne brushed past them and took a path that looked oddly foreign and yet familiar simultaneously. "Here." She stopped and knelt beside a small stone and caressed its weathered edges with her hand. "My Thomas died because of magic, so the ground here will be fertile. Besides, I'm sure he'd be happy to know he's able to help undo the abomination I created with my lover." She ducked her head in silent commune before going to work arranging her bones.

"What's next?" Colin stood back from the bones, never getting too close to the makeshift altar.

"I'm not sure." Jason shrugged, then sank his hands deep into his pockets. Reassured the vial was still within a fingers reach, he exhaled a breath he hadn't realized he was holding. "But whatever's next, I think we should be on guard."

"For what?"

"The worst of the worst? The dealer of ultimate pain and devastation? The ultimate deceiver?" He ticked the names off one finger at a time.

"The devil? For real?" Colin's eyes grew wide.

"Dema isn't *the* devil," Delila chastised. "It's the title humans best attribute to him. He does have a temper and was assigned to guard the Underworld because of his proclivities, but he isn't inherently evil." Delila laid her skull at the head the skeleton she'd constructed. "If only I'd listened to him. Maybe this wouldn't be happening." Regret lanced through her words, sharp and sure. "Stand back," she ordered, as she poured a circle of salt around the circumference of the overlaid graves. "I'll need you to chant with me."

A pointed glare lanced through him and landed with the thud of realization. Jason gripped Colin's arm and pulled him close. "Whatever happens, don't believe anything the two of them say. I'm not sure they can be trusted," he said under his breath.

Colin nodded and took another step back. Delila began chanting in monotone syllables and Jason joined in. The wind kicked up, sending Daphne's long dark locks into a frenzy around her face. It was eerie seeing the woman in such a state, knowing another being sat in the driver's seat of her body. Jason cracked his knuckles and braced for whatever may come their way.

The birds in the surrounding trees took flight all at once as if they could sense the evil roaring down some invisible tracks from Hell toward them. Above the bones appeared a door, much like the one he'd encountered at the Dews which led to the apothecary, but this one opened more like a wound.

The being on the other side squeezed through. Alone.

Birthed into reality on this plane.

Swaddled in a dark cloud, the being seeped around the bones laid at where his feet should be and searched the field. Looking for what, Jason couldn't be sure. The being's ghostly presence unnerved him. He shouldn't be seeing him if he was a ghost—it wasn't among his gifts. And yet, the being before him wasn't solid, whole, human. Jason swallowed the lump in his throat. The devil shouldn't be in a ghostly form.

Dema's eyes set upon Daphne then lit with recognition. "Delila," his deep voice rumbled. He reached a blurry hand toward her but was met with resistance as it neared the salted border. "My love. Why won't you come near?"

Daphne's shoulders went rigid. "Who is this Delila?" she challenged.

"Ah, my love, I'd recognize your spirit anywhere in any realm. Don't betray me again."

The devil's words were said to be cajoling, but the sharp tone wasn't lost on Jason.

"We've summoned you here today to help deal with your son," Jason broke the silence that lingered between the two as they faced off against one another in a silent game of tug-of-war. "We need to know how he can be defeated before he continues to wreak havoc on the people of this plane."

"Ah. Drammelech. I've thought of him every day for many years. But never as fondly as I've thought of you." He stared into Daphne's eyes and ignored Jason and Colin. "I beg of you, my love. Allow me to touch you. To kiss you. To feel the

81

softness of your skin beneath me."

When Delila ignored his request, the incorporeal devil turned toward Colin and crooked a finger at him.

"Don't you move." Jason grabbed Colin's arm and tugged as the man's feet took a step toward the salt circle.

"He's free to do as he wishes," the devil murmured. "He's a being with free will."

Jason pulled harder against Colin's forward motion as unsuccessfully as a gnat pushing a boulder up the side of a mountain. Before he could stop him, Colin's foot breached the salt, tearing an opening in the protective barrier between the devil and the rest of the world.

A sly smile whisked across the devil's face. He reached a hand to Colin, and before he could move another step, the devil's essence made contact with his skin and disappeared.

"No." Daphne's cry shattered the quiet, her eyes rounded on Jason, wide, afraid. "This can't be happening," she sobbed.

It was the first time since the séance that Jason wondered if he was talking to Delila or the real Daphne.

TWELVE

A SHOWDOWN WAS inevitable. Jason knew it to be true more than anything else. He stared at the man and woman standing before him in the small family cemetery and weighed his options. If the devil had taken residence in Colin's body, as Delila had almost certainly done in Daphne's, the two might be his best weapons against the devil holding Callie hostage. Resigned to the situation, he turned to Colin.

"Can you still drive?"

Question marks danced across his face before he answered with a slow, cautious, "Yes."

Jason turned to Daphne, hoping Delila hadn't vacated her body when her former lover had appeared. "Is there anything else you needed before we leave?"

She turned an uneasy gaze on Colin, shook her

head, and stepped closer to Jason. "We have everything we need."

"Good. Let's go catch ourselves a devil."

Colin grunted but fell into step behind them as they made their way back to his truck. "How should we go about finding Drammelech? I'm sure he won't be sitting around waiting for us."

"Agreed," Jason nodded. "But I have an idea. With a witch in his arsenal, he'll need a place with magical significance, too. And we've kept him out of the Dews and here, so the most obvious place would be the bed and breakfast. Teresa locked away a lot of spirits there, and her magic surely still lingers. Do either of you know how to get there?" He paused and turned toward the couple behind him. Dammit. Colin and Daphne's hands clasped tight and their bodies leaned into one another.

When both seemed confused, he ground his teeth against the anger welling inside of him. This was exactly what he didn't need—a love-struck couple back for a second chance at love. He shook his head and willed himself to not erupt.

"Tap into the memories of your hosts then. We need to get there before your son does something irreversible to Callie." Venom clung to his razor sharp words and his nails dug deep into his flesh with every irritated second ticking by.

When they reached the truck, Colin climbed behind the wheel as if it was the most natural thing he'd done all day, and Daphne slid onto the bench beside him with a dainty hand laid on his thigh. Jason angled himself into the cab beside her and hoped he could remember the roads taken into town. If he could remember those, then he'd be able to orient himself enough to find Teresa's former home.

*****

With only a few missed turns, the three arrived at the B & B after nine o'clock. The sun was still steadily rising in the sky, and with each progressive move toward their target, animals, people, even insects seemed to scurry elsewhere in a hurry. The battle to come vibrated through the air surrounding them, palpable, potent, paralyzing. This might very well be the end of his existence after being imprisoned for so long, and yet, Jason couldn't look past the man holding Callie hostage.

They pulled to the curb in front of the B & B and filed out onto the sidewalk. From the vantage point the wrap around porch offered, Jason peered into the glass panes until he located what he desperately wanted to find. Callie. Perched on a chair, weariness hung from her shoulders.

"Psst," he hissed at her, hoping the devil wasn't nearby.

She turned and faced him, pale, her lips parted in silent warning, anxiety coming off her in waves. She shook her head from side to side and closed her eyes against the sight of him. When they opened, the light behind them was gone; her body mimicking an empty shell.

"So I sssssssee you've returned."

The unmistakable stutter said all he needed to know.

"Come inside. And bring your friends with you." The devil stepped into the room and placed his hands on Callie's shoulders. "It's nice to see you decided to bring me what I wanted." The devil cocked his head to the side and a wicked grin snaked across his face.

Jason nodded and made his way back to the front door where Daphne and Colin stood with a set of matching question marks written on their faces.

"He's inside and Callie's with him."

"Then it's time," Delila declared and reached for the doorknob.

"Not so fast, my love." Colin reached out a hand and pressed it onto hers. "Our son might respond better if we don't show our true natures. He's convinced himself we can't be trusted."

Jason studied the exchange and debated his options. There weren't an abundance of choices if he stood a chance at saving Callie. He pushed in front of Delila/Daphne and grasped the knob. It was now or never.

The path to the sitting room was one he knew well. Like so many years ago, he found malevolence in the room instead of warmth and love, only this time, the evil stood front and center, its presence suffocating.

The devil beckoned Callie to him, and Jason's hand twitched at his side as the urge to spell the demon became downright painful. He hadn't paid attention to her fully since he entered the room, but now she moved to his windowpane. The frame of his former prison held fast to a few jagged teeth of colored glass and was possibly her last ditch effort. Indecision flickered across her face before she succumbed to the devil's wishes.

The indecision imprinted on her face worried him. In the brief amount of time that he knew her, she'd always been steadfast in her facial features, but now she looked uncertain. He turned his attention back to the biggest threat in the room and glared. Elech had done this to them, made them fight one another all in the hopes that Daphne could be saved. But Jason knew the truth. She couldn't be saved. Destiny in the form of the devil would continue to haunt her until she broke down and accepted her place within the sequence of events she was meant to play. Which meant one of two things would happen today. Either Elech would get Daphne and the rest of them would walk away with a tenuous future at best, or, and his money was on this one, he'd take her and the rest would perish. Of the two options, Jason could only accept one. Unfortunately, it was the one Callie might never forgive him for choosing.

"I've done as you asked." Jason inclined his head toward the entryway behind him. "See for yourself. The one you want waits for you. She's come willingly and understands this trade will result in the safe return of her friend."

Callie's eyes went wide, disbelief and hatred warred for rights as the dominant emotion. "No," she whimpered.

"It's the only way," Jason chided.

"You promised."

"I promised to do everything I could. We stepped too far past what I could do." Jason ducked his head to avoid meeting her eyes. He couldn't handle knowing as every word sank into her, she fought the urge to kill him.

"You're a liar," she seethed. "Just like the rest of them."

The footfalls of Daphne and Colin sounded behind him. It was time.

"I'm sorry, Calliope Jane."

Her brows knit with confusion. Jason used the split second to take a deep breath, calm his nerves, and rip the remaining shards of glass from the window and send them flying through the air at both Callie and the devil. She screamed as the shards pierced her skin, and the devil howled in matching agony. Her face crumpled as the hand she'd been holding behind her back fell to her side in a bloody mess, a large glass shard tumbling from it onto the floor.

"Why?" Callie whimpered, and her knees fell to the floor.

"I had no choice," he explained. Jason pulled the *Reveal* vial from his pocket and uncorked the top. "Forgive me," he called toward Callie. He turned and faced Daphne and Colin. "Drink this. Please."

When neither made a move to take the vial, he jerked his hand toward Colin and some of the liquid splashed out of the vial on onto the man's skin. Colin's face twisted in confusion as the potion on his skin began to smoke. Realization flashed across his face as his glare landed on Jason. Colin dropped to the floor and an odd snapping sound echoed in the room as his body began contorting and configuring into first a brown bear, then shrinking into the body of a squirrel, all within the span of less than a minute.

Colin's shape shifting was unlike anything Jason had ever witnessed in all his dealings with the magical world. In his last solid formation, Colin took on the body of a large chocolate colored dog, howled, and then shifted into a warm mocha-tinged cloud. Because having the King of the Underworld trapped inside a fucking cloud was exactly what Jason needed right now.

Shit. He rubbed his eyes and hoped when he opened them again it would all be a crazy hallucination. Nope. *Damn.* It could only mean one thing—Colin was one of the fabled Elementals. And the devil was locked inside his... his what? *Cloud?*

"You imbecile. What've you done?" Daphne shuddered as the cloud rolled over her bared skin and put a tentative hand through it.

"He's made my job much easier," the devil taunted. "Despite your attempt to stop me, I'll honor our agreement. Her," he pointed at Daphne, "for her."

Jason fixed his eyes on Callie. She whimpered on the ground, no longer trying to find the points of glass sticking into her flesh. What hurt him the most was her staunch refusal to look at him.

"Agreed." His answer was a whisper, but it was all the devil required. Jason swung around toward Daphne and hoped his theory regarding Delila's inability to use magic in Daphne's body wasn't in his head. He plucked the vial of *Command* he'd been keeping in his trousers since his first trip into the apothecary, and held it out toward Daphne. "Drink this willingly and you'll live. Fight and I won't be able to protect you."

Daphne's hand took the little bottle from him and brought it to her nose to sniff. With accusation in her glare, she shook her head.

"Please. For her. She's already given so much for you. And this is how you can repay her," Jason begged.

Without a word, she tipped the blue-tinted contents of the jar past her lips and swallowed. "Are you happy?" She scowled.

"Very," he agreed. "Now, go to him. Trust that he won't hurt you if you do as he asks."

Daphne's eyes glazed over, indicating the potion had worked with efficient effectiveness, blocking any magic Delila might conjure to the contrary.

"Go to him," he repeated, this time louder, controlled, confident. As she passed by, Jason grabbed her hand and tucked the opened vial of *Reveal* in her hand. "You know what to do," he murmured in her ear as he pressed a small hug to her body.

When Daphne reached the devil's side, the monster's tongue flicked between his teeth, tasting the air around him. It was then she doused him with the contents of the jar.

The devil hissed and sputtered. Indignation ran across his face. "You evil bitch!" His face contorted, his body slumped, and the sound of fabric tearing echoed in the room. While the devil doubled over, squealing in pain like a pig about to be slaughtered, Jason yelled "come," to Daphne. With the *Command* tonic still in play, she did as told while he gathered Callie into his arms. Together, the three of them, and Colin's clouded visage left the B & B not daring to turn back.

THIRTEEN

THE CONTENTS OF the vial caused more pain than
the window shards. The prospect of death crossed
Drammelech's mind until he remembered himself.
He *was* death.

The torment ripping through his back as his
true nature tore the flesh of his human form, forced
him to his knees. He lived a couple hundred years
without undergoing this change. Until now. Until
them. *The Barrens.*

Hatred coursed through him on the tail of his
transition. He'd been certain Daphne would
succumb like her mother. But she was strong.
Almost as if she was driven by something more
than courage.

His clothes lay in tattered puddles at his feet
unable to contain his devilish form. Large wings,
shaped like those of a bat, but covered in feathers

wrapped around his body and warmed him. His tail flickered in the air behind him as he rewound the last few minutes in his mind again.

Daphne approaching him. Submission etched on her face. No. Not submission. *Resistance*. She had been walking to him against he will.

Impossible.

Unless…

Unless the glimmer in Daphne's eyes, the one which had screamed his mother's name, hadn't been some phantom passing resemblance.

Delila.

The witch who started this.

She was back.

And it would end with her. He would ensure it with every ounce of his strength.

She would not stop him this time.

He spread his wings and launched himself into the night sky. He needed to prepare for the war about to come.

The End

FIRE'S REVENGE SNIPPET

IF YOU THOUGHT Elech's evilness could only be contained to one series, you'd be wrong. Take a peek into *Fire's Revenge*, the first novel in a series featuring elementals, witches, and our favorite devil.

FIRE'S REVENGE

ONE
OVERWORLD
CIRCA 1725

Fate knew her job as pseudo-deity was important and she took it as seriously as a being in the Overworld could. That was until, one half-devil-half-witch waltzed into the Overworld uninvited and stole a precious artifact.

With a charming face and smooth talking words, the young devil-witch dazzled Fate. It had been so long since the last time she had actually conversed with another. The ideas of a visit from a being that could walk through the veils that kept humans from the Overworld and Underworld played on her heartstrings; played them like a master composer.

Their time together was brief. In his first visit she only learned his name: Drammelech; Elech as his family called him. She offered him her title in lieu of her name: Fate. He had flashed her a wide smile with the hint of a dimple at its corner and said that she must have known he'd come for her. She laughed off his flirty nature and relished the time they spoke.

He brought her a single fluffy pink flower on his next visit.

"What is this?"

"Rue."

"Rue? Why would you bring me something with such a sad connotation attached to its name?" Fate studied the young man before her.

"Because I rue that I cannot have you in my everyday life. Your beauty speaks to me in a way that nothing in my realm ever has." Bashful eyes lowered, punctuating his proclamation with the light stain of red that colored his cheeks.

It was in that one simple confession that her heart filled as it never had before. She took great pains to make sure every moment of their time together was well spent; full of laughter, conversation, and genuine happiness. On one particular visit, when Elech asked to see more than the main chamber of her Overworld post, she didn't hesitate before taking him into her most favorite room; the records room.

She led him into the vault where every being's scroll was kept under lock and key. It reminded her of the warehouses that her charges were so keen on using to store useless baubles and tokens. The difference was that this chamber was unending.

The day she had taken over for the previous soul, she had been shown into this very chamber of vastness that seemed larger than anything she could comprehend. She recalled asking in a hushed tone how big the chamber was. The look on her predecessor's face was enough of an answer that no more words had been needed.

In her years, she had tried to understand the organization of the vast room, but she had yet to figure out the magical system to the order of the scrolls. Although, the easiest to find belonged to the mystical beings which lived among the humans. Those scrolls always appeared near the front of the shelves and often had brightly colored symbols on the exterior of the rolled parchment.

With every falling grain of sand in the constantly flowing hourglass that mimicked the time of her charges, scrolls would appear or disappear as if they had always been as they were with the next drop. She oftentimes wondered if the disappearing scrolls reappeared elsewhere in the cavernous chamber, but to venture forth in search of them would take longer than she could spare. In the turn of her back, turmoil could erupt amongst her charges since time in the Overworld didn't work the same as it did on Earth. With that in mind, her forays into this chamber were typically the highlight of her time spent in the Overworld.

Fate stepped aside and allowed Elech into this sacred space. It gave her a sense of joy to be able to share this place with someone. The majestic nature of it all never failed to take her breath away and she wanted so much to see her joy reflected in his piercing eyes. She watched, rapt, as a wash of emotions rolled over his handsome face.

"What is this place?" Awe laced every word.

"I call it the chamber of records." She fingered the delicate shell of the hourglass. "This is where the universe balances. Within the scrolls, there is a tenuous balance struck between light, dark, old, new, beginnings, and endings."

Elech walked farther into the room and ran a hand along a row housing mounds of scrolls. His fingers settled on one and slipped it from the shelf. With gentle fingers, he unrolled the parchment and scanned it.

"What if this scroll were to get misplaced?" He rerolled the record and held it between his thumb and forefinger like it might burn him.

"It mustn't." Fate moved toward him and snatched the scroll from his grasp. "This single scroll represents the life of one of my charges and if something were to change, another scroll would surely appear to act as balance." She gently slid the scroll back into its place on the shelf.

Elech nodded and walked back to the main opening in the chamber. Beside the hourglass was a podium that held the largest tome the world never knew existed. Its leather wrapped spine was the glue that held all of Earth's existence together. Tucked into the pages of the book laid the blade of the most powerful item in the chamber: Fate's dagger. Her predecessor had gone to great lengths to reiterate the importance of keeping it hidden away, and now his words resurfaced in the forefront of her mind as Elech drew closer and closer to its resting place. An item of such power could be used to do so much damage in the world in the wrong hands, but in hers it was the instrument to set things gone awry on a corrected path. A sigh left her lips as Elech inspected the hourglass.

Fate watched the steady trickle of sand and moved to her left. She fingered the thick leather-bound tome that was home to a list of names and slid the jeweled silver hilt from between the book's pages. It felt heavy in her hand as she tucked it into the garter beneath her long flowing skirt. The knowledge that it was safe gave her a sense of peace.

Elech's next visit was years later even though the time passed in seemingly the blink of an eye. This time when he came to her, he appeared a full grown man even though she knew his age to still be young by her charges' standards. Instead of another pink fluffy rue, he held in his hand a long stemmed white rose.

"I thought you might've forgotten me," she remarked as she accepted his offering.

"Never."

His voice was deep, full-bodied, and sent a chill racing down her spine. When his hands slid down her arms, an actual shiver sliced through her body. How long had it been since she had felt the touch of another? Long before being assigned to her current post, that's for sure. She arched into him, pleased to find him hard and angular beneath her wanton fingers. In the space of a breath he had her in his arms, hands scorching over her exposed skin until fabric balled into his eager hands. His mouth, warm on her chaste lips, tasted like sunshine and a warm summer's breeze.

Fate threw caution and all her dignity into the wind and succumbed to Elech. With each tantalizing touch of his fingers against her flesh, she basked in the sensations of seduction. The anomaly of a fluttering in her chest that had earned her this post, kicked up as his tentative touches became more determined on their trail up her thighs beneath her skirt. She closed her eyes and cherished the intimacy of her predicament until a tug sent her eyes wide. The cool blade of the dagger she wore in the garter against her thigh sliced though her delicate flesh in a rush of warm, sticky liquid. Before she could defend herself, the press of the blade against her throat halted any further movement.

"I hate to do this," Elech whispered in her ear. "But you are the only thing standing between me and greatness." He pressed his lips to hers in a final kiss as the blade dug into her skin once more, this time slicing across her throat until it became hard to breathe. The fluttering in her chest that made her more human than ethereal catapulted, racing toward a finish line she could no longer sense. Elech stood, wiped the broad side of the blade against his trousers and blinked out of the realm.

Without her to dictate the course of human existence, chaos was sure to ensue, but protecting her charges from whatever evil Elech planned was more important. With her last breaths, she dragged herself into the chamber of records and sealed the doors behind her with all of her remaining magic. Now he would need more than just his smooth words to get into the chamber. Satisfied with her fortitude and forethought, she crumpled into a heap on the floor, knocking scrolls about on her way down. As much as she wanted to retrieve them and put them right again, she no longer had the strength. She stared at the scattered rolls of parchment, most decorated with symbols she knew instinctively. The mess on the floor would surely change the course of life for her beloved charges, but how, she could only guess.

Her last thought flashed through her brain on the fading embers of light in her soul. "What have I done?"

Available now for purchase where ebooks are sold.

WANT A SNEAK PEEK AT WHAT'S COMING

NEXT FOR ELECH?

IF YOU CAN'T get enough of your favorite devil, visit
www.jeniburns.com for news regarding upcoming
releases.

BIOGRAPHY

JENI BURNS is a Jersey girl living in a southern world. While she's firmly planted in the South with her husband, two kids, and one massive poodle, her heart still lives in the Northwestern part of New Jersey where her characters reside. Since writing about home is cheaper than airfare, she spends much of her time living vicariously in NJ's snowy winters and humidity-free summers.

Jeni has been telling stories since she first learned to string two words together. Thanks to her mom and her middle school English teacher both telling her she should be a writer; she now happily spends her days writing all the stories that continuously float around in her head while drinking fabulous decaf coffees.